THE HEEL OF ACHILLES

THE
HEEL OF ACHILLES

E. M. DELAFIELD

WILDSIDE PRESS

**To YOÉ: my sister, and always
my greatest friend.**

*"Provinces twain o'er the land held sway, and the
	country was ruled by twain,
I made the laws, as King, but you, as Premier, revoked
	them again.
You were my faithful A.D.C., when I was the Captain
	bold,
But Watson I, to your Sherlock Holmes, in the Baker
	Street days of old.
We went through times that were strange and bad, and
	we shared and shared the same,
And talked and dreamed and planned of the day when
	we'd come to freedom and fame.
And the dreams came true, and the times were
	changed, and we did the things we'd planned—
(Don't you remember the two Fur Coats, and the trips
	to Weston sand?)—
So now you work at a real Career, and I'm writing, in
	Singapore,
And send my book to my Twin—a token of all that has
	gone before.
A sign of the past—but a symbol, too, that is known to
	you and me,
Of the days together still to come, and the best that is
	yet to be."*

I

"I am an orphan," reflected Lydia Raymond, with immense satisfaction.

She was a very intelligent little girl of twelve years old, and she remembered very well that when her father had died out in China, three years ago, it was her mother who had been the centre of attention and compassion. People had spoken about her poor dead father, and had praised him and pitied him, but their real attention had all been for the widow, who was there under their eyes, pathetic and sorrow-stricken. Lydia herself had been "poor little thing," but Grandpapa and her aunts and uncle had all told her that it was her mother who must be thought of now, and she knew that they kept on saying to one another that "the child will be a comfort to poor Mary." Her own individuality, which she felt so strongly, did not seem to count at all, and Lydia had, quite silently, resented that intensely, ever since she could remember anything at all.

Once her mother had read her some extracts of old letters from her dead father, letters which had once come so regularly every week in thin blue envelopes with the Hong Kong postmark.

"Kiss our baby Lydia for me. I hope she is a good little thing always ... some day, when these years of hard work are over, you won't have to sacrifice yourself any more, my poor Mary...." And, later on, in the last letter of all: "The child's life is only a continuation of ours, my Mary."

Long afterwards, Lydia, who never forgot the words, came to see them as the expression of man's eternal wistful attempt to live on in the generation supplanting his own, but when her mother read them aloud to her, in a voice choked with tears, something in Lydia revolted violently.

"My life is my own," she thought stubbornly, "not just a continuation of somebody else's."

With that acute clarity of vision that enabled her to analyze certain aspects of her childhood's world with such astonishing maturity, she once told herself:

"They don't love me for myself at all. Grandpapa doesn't love me the least bit—he doesn't love anybody. And mother loves me because I'm *her* child, and the aunts love me because I'm father's child, and they think I'm a comfort to mother."

She could hardly remember her father, and though at first she had shed tears over his death, Lydia had quickly dried them.

"Now, dear, you must be a good little girl and not cry and make poor mother more unhappy than she is already," had said harassed-looking Aunt Evelyn. "You know you must think of her now. You'll have to be her comfort."

And almost immediately afterwards Aunt Evelyn had said to Lydia's mother:

"Do, do give way and cry, dearie. It will be so much better for you. I know you're wonderful, but you'll suffer for it later on. You're bound to."

After that it had not needed Aunt Evelyn's further observation that "poor little Lydia didn't know what her loss meant" to dry Lydia's perfunctory tears with the sting of an inflexible pride.

She would not cry again until they were prepared to concede to her the major right to affliction!

She did not love her mother very much. It is more common than is generally allowed, for an intelligent child, still in bondage to her natural instinct, reinforced by the tradition of allegiance to natural authorities, to couple that allegiance with a perfectly distinct antipathy to the personality of either or both parents. Lydia's dislike of her mother's sentimentality, her constant vacillation of purpose, and her incessant garrulity, was only unchildlike in her calm analysis of it, and in the conscious restraint that she put upon it.

Mrs. Raymond had often said, sometimes in Lydia's hearing, that she would welcome death.

"But for little Lydia, I think I should have put an end to it all long ago. But how can I leave her, when she only has me?"

Mrs. Raymond, however, without any intervention of her own, when Lydia was twelve years old, reached the haven to which, since her husband's death, she had so often aspired.

"I am an orphan."

Lydia, already a dignified and self-contained little girl, bore herself with a new, pale composure.

It was for her that Aunt Evelyn, once more summoned from her shabby, untidy house at Wimbledon, was now hastily ordering mourning, and to whom the Wimbledon cousins had written brief, blotted letters of compassion and sympathy, and it was her future that Aunt Evelyn and Uncle George and Aunt Beryl had all been discussing under their breath whenever they thought she was not listening.

This, at least, was Lydia's complacent conviction, until she overheard a few chance words about Grandpapa, and how best they could break it to him, when he was old, and his heart was weak—and he had, besides, never really got over the shock of poor Peter's death, three years ago.

So it was Grandpapa they were thinking of now!

Lydia really felt very angry. Grandpapa, however, did not exact an undue amount of attention, on the whole.

"Grandpapa is old," said Aunt Beryl, with a hint of apology in her voice. "Very old people don't realize things quite in the same way—they're more familiar with grief, perhaps."

"The real blow was poor Peter's death," said Aunt Evelyn, also determined that Grandpapa should be accredited with his due meed of afflictions.

Aunt Beryl, who lived with Grandpapa, took Lydia to stay with them.

They had a house at the seaside, only two hours by train from London, and Aunt Evelyn came with them, ostensibly to see how Grandpapa was, but in reality, Lydia felt certain, in order to help them to decide upon her own future.

The two aunts talked to one another in anxious undertones all through the journey; their two, almost identical, black hats nodding so close together that Aunt Beryl's hard straw brim kept on knocking against Aunt Evelyn's stiff, upstanding bow of rigid crape. Although the younger one was still unmarried, Lydia's two aunts had never lost a certain indefinable similarity of taste that always made them look as though they were dressed alike.

Aunt Evelyn was Mrs. Senthoven.

"You can remember it because of Beethoven," she always said, with a nervous laugh. She had three children, and was several years older than her sister.

Miss Raymond might have been handsome in a small, beaky way but for her extreme thinness and the permanent anxiety in her light-brown eyes. "Beryl is the youngest bird in the old home nest, and is always with dear Grandpapa," Aunt Evelyn and Uncle George were apt to say.

The youngest bird in the old home nest, growing yearly more pinched and vulture-like, invariably acquiesced eagerly in the pious formula, and thus enabled Aunt Evelyn to give her undivided attention to the straitened, clamorous household at Wimbledon, and Uncle George to leave his room in Grandpapa's house untenanted during his fortnightly holiday from the office.

Now, however, he was at home, having gone straight back after the funeral. He met them at the station.

Uncle George was small and fair, with a habit of asking thoughtful questions of the kind apt to provoke hasty and inaccurate replies, which he then had the satisfaction of correcting.

He said, "Well, well, Lydia," and gave her a little, awkward pat on the shoulder, that she quite understood to be expressive of his pity and sympathy.

"What about the 'bus?" said Aunt Beryl.

"No, no," Aunt Evelyn protested quickly. "The walk would do us good. No need to take the 'bus."

This was one of the fundamental differences between the aunts and Lydia's mother. Mrs. Raymond had always taken a cab from the station, whether she had brought any luggage or no, when she came down to see Grandpapa. She had never seemed to be aware, as Lydia had privately always been aware, that the household in Regency Terrace thought very much the worse of her for the extravagance.

"The 'bus could take your bag, Evelyn. I know the man," said Uncle George. "It will be quite all right." He put out his hand for the small, dirty, brown suit-case that was weighing his sister down on one side.

"Well—I don't know," she hesitated. "I suppose it will be sixpence or more saved, if we carry it ourselves." She laughed nervously.

"Better let the 'bus take it. I can say a word to the conductor," persisted Uncle George, now burdened with the bag.

"Oh, it isn't far. I think I'd rather keep an eye on it."

"Just as you like."

Uncle George raised his eyebrows, and they trudged away down the dusty station road.

Lydia was tired and hot in her new, fussy black clothes, and the contrast between her present discomfort and those condemned, self-indulgent ways of her mother, in the advantages of which she had always shared, brought a genuine realization of loss to her mind with a dull pang.

"What made your train late?" Uncle George inquired, patiently shifting the suit-case into his other hand.

"Was it late?"

"Surely. Wasn't it, Beryl?"

"I think it *was*. About five or ten minutes."

Her brother immediately looked astonished.

"Five *or* ten! The railway company would tell you that there is a very great difference. As a matter of fact, your train came in exactly seven-and-a-half minutes behind time."

"Perhaps we started late," wearily suggested Mrs. Senthoven. She was beginning to limp a little in her tight, black boots.

"Not very likely to do that. Probably you lost time at the Junction. The two-fifteen always has to wait about there. I've noticed it."

"Probably that was it," said Aunt Beryl, with tired acquiescence in the masculine infallibility on the subject of time-tables.

"I expect it was that. Let me see—you would have stopped only once before the Junction——"

The discussion, if it could be called one, when the only wish of the aunts was obviously to agree with Uncle George, lasted all the way to Regency Terrace.

Then Aunt Evelyn and Aunt Beryl both said, "Here we are!" and Uncle George put the suit-case down upon the lowest step of the stone flight that led to the front door as though by no possible feat of endurance could he have sustained its weight further.

"There's Grandpapa," said Mrs. Senthoven, looking up at a first-floor window, and nodding vigorously.

"George!" exclaimed Aunt Beryl reproachfully, "why is Grandpapa in the drawing-room? You know he always sits in the dining-room on week-days. With the parrot to keep him company and all."

Her brother was spared the necessity of providing any explanation as to Grandpapa's disregard of his privileges by the opening of the front door.

"Welcome, my dear child," said Aunt Beryl very kindly to Lydia, and she kissed her.

Then she looked round sharply at the servant who had opened the door. Her face relaxed at the immaculate cap and apron that met her gaze, and she said graciously:

"Good afternoon, Gertrude."

As they went into the dining-room, of which the door already stood open, Lydia heard Aunt Beryl say in tones of satisfaction:

"The girl really is improving at last. I've had such a time with her!"

"I wish I could get our girl at home to look half so smart," said Aunt Evelyn, shaking her head. "But she's got more than she can manage, with the house in the morning, and then the waiting at meals—Robert absolutely insists on that—and half her time she doesn't dress in the afternoons at all, and I really can't blame her. Just goes to the door with her arms all turned up, anyhow. Not that we have many callers," sighed Aunt Evelyn. "I've had to give over social life altogether, practically; the children take such a lot of see-

11

ing to. Don't ever marry a poor man, Beryl."

The fiction still prevailed between the sisters that a choice of matrimonial projects lay ever before Miss Raymond.

"If you ladies have finished talking secrets——" said Uncle George, in reproachful reference to the rapid undertones employed by Lydia's aunts.

"Yes, now what about Grandpapa?"

"He'll want to see our little Lydia."

"Poor child! Get her a little wine and a biscuit first, George."

Lydia sat complacently at the square dining-room table, whilst Uncle George slowly unlocked the lower half of the sideboard and brought out a decanter with a very little red liquid in it, and Aunt Beryl produced, also from a locked receptacle, a small glass barrel containing three or four Albert biscuits.

"You sit here quietly, dear. Aunt Evelyn and I will go up to Grandpapa first."

The aunts left the room together, and Lydia and Uncle George remained solemnly facing one another across the dining-room table. Lydia was much too self-possessed a little girl ever to feel any necessity for making conversation, and as her uncle remained silent, she occupied herself in gazing round the dining-room, familiar though it was to her already. The table was still covered with rather worn red baize; Grandpapa's arm-chair, in which Grandpapa should by rights have been sitting now, still stood in the bay window, flanked by the small, round table which supported the parrot's cage. The cage was covered with an old piece of green stuff now, and Lydia was glad of it. She was not at all fond of the parrot. Over the mantelpiece hung "The Monarch of the Glen," and over the writing-table, at which no one ever wrote, but where Aunt Beryl did a good deal of sewing, was "Derby Day." Lydia had heard Aunt Evelyn say that the detail in that picture always struck her as being quite wonderful.

The sideboard was the largest piece of furniture in the room, and it occupied almost the whole of one end of it. Lydia had often been told the story of the sideboard's arrival at Regency Terrace—the impossibility of getting it in at the front door—Uncle George's humorous suggestion that the roof of the house should be taken off—and finally its lengthy and strenuous entrance through a window, assisted by a large crane. It was a matter of everlasting regret to Lydia that this sensational progress should have taken place some twenty years before her own arrival into the world. In front of the empty grate stood a faded worked screen, its spiral legs embedded in the fluffy black hearth-rug.

"Oh," said Lydia, suddenly reminded, "where is Shamrock?"

"Out, I suppose," said Uncle George simply. Shamrock was Grandpapa's dog, and Uncle George had good reason to disclaim all responsibility for Shamrock's in-comings and out-goings.

"A seaside town, or, in fact, any town, is no place for a dog, in my opinion," said Uncle George.

"Of course they have more fun in the country," glibly returned his niece, who had never spent more than three consecutive days in the country anywhere, nor owned a dog in her life. "They can run after chickens and lambs, I suppose," she added innocently.

"They can indeed!" ejaculated Uncle George. "But why lambs, Lydia?"

"I thought I'd seen pictures of dogs running after sheep, and barking at them to make them go the right way."

"Sheep-dog! That's another matter. Sheep are not lambs, child—nor is this the season for lambs."

Uncle George looked happier, having found an opportunity for the bestowal of information.

Lydia secretly thought him very like Mr. Barlow in "Sandford and Merton," and had no idea that her comparison was anything but complimentary.

"Have you ever read 'Sandford and Merton,' Uncle George?" she inquired conversationally. She had no idea of simulating a conventional grief for her mother with Uncle George, knowing instinctively that any such display would merely embarrass him. Uncle George liked one to be intelligent and very attentive to everything he said. Lydia had often asked him questions, the answers to which left her profoundly indifferent, merely for the sake of pleasing him. Her unconsciously cynical acknowledgment to herself of her own motives at least saved her from the charge of insincerity.

Lydia had seen so little of her grandfather during the last three years that she could not remember what he liked from little girls, although she retained a vivid impression, mostly gathered from her mother, that Aunt Evelyn's noisy, slangy, hockey-playing Beatrice and Olive were not approved of by him.

Lydia, the precocious little only child of a mother half-enviously and half-contemptuously acknowledged to be "rather a fine lady" by the Raymonds and the Senthovens, was not likely to transgress in the same directions as Beatrice and Olive.

When Aunt Evelyn appeared at the dining-room door with her summons, Lydia followed her demurely upstairs. She remembered the steep, rather narrow staircase, with a blue carpet that gave place abruptly on the second flight to yellow oilcloth, and the ugly blue paper on the walls, quite well.

The drawing-room seemed altogether strange to her, but she was given no time to examine it.

"Here is little Lydia, Grandpapa," said Aunt Beryl, who stood as though on guard behind the arm-chair in the bow window, that looked out on to a distant strip of grey sea.

How *tiny* Grandpapa was!

It quite shocked Lydia to see the minute proportions of the stiff little figure that sat back rigidly in the depths of the arm-chair.

Grandpapa's hand was like a claw, and his eyes looked out of a network of wrinkles such as Lydia had never seen or imagined on a human countenance.

She half expected his voice to be in proportion, but it was in very sharp, incisive tones that he addressed her:

"How d'y do, my dear? You are very young to know grief."

"Lydia has been very good and brave, and given us no trouble at all, Grandpapa," said Aunt Beryl.

"That's right. That's quite right. How old are you, Lyddie?"

Lydia suddenly remembered that her grandfather had always called her "Lyddie," although no one else ever did so.

"Twelve and a half, Grandpapa."

"Can you read?"

"Oh, yes," said Lydia, astonished.

"There is reading *and* reading," said the old man rather grimly. "If yours is very good you can read to me in the mornings, and save your Aunt Beryl."

"We shall have to see about some lessons for her in the mornings," said Aunt Beryl rather repressively.

"Eh, what's that? You don't want to go to school, do you, my dear?"

Lydia wanted to go to school very much, and had always resented her mother's refusal to send her there, and the irregular, desultory lessons at home, from which she knew that she learnt nothing useful.

But already she felt certain that to say so would not advance her cause with Grandpapa.

"I have never been to school," she said at last.

"A very good thing too. I don't like all this business of girls trying to be like boys, and learning all sorts of rough ways."

Old Raymond cast a malicious glance at his daughter Evelyn, whose two girls attended a high school.

"You're tired, Grandpapa," she said gently and unresentfully, although she coloured.

"What made you sit in the drawing-room to-day?" asked Aunt Beryl. "You know you always stay in the dining-room until six o'clock."

Grandpapa's perfectly alert old face suddenly assumed a blank expression.

"Eh, my dear?" he said vacantly.

Aunt Beryl repeated the observation in a higher key.

"I can't hear you," said Grandpapa obstinately.

Aunt Evelyn and Aunt Beryl exchanged glances.

"Don't do that, my dears, it's very ill-bred. Even little Lyddie here can tell you that. Very bad manners to exchange glances. I suppose you thought I couldn't see you, but I've got very good eyes yet."

The old man chuckled gaily at the discomfiture on the faces of the two women.

"You must come downstairs now, Grandpapa. It's tea-time," said Aunt Beryl firmly.

Lydia wondered how anyone so very old and frail could ever be taken downstairs. Did Uncle George carry him? She saw with horror that neither of her aunts made any move to assist him as he leant forward and gripped a stout stick that stood against the arm-chair.

Then he began to slide down the seat of the deep chair, his old frame quite rigid, one hand clutching the arm of the chair, the other the stick.

"Oh!" cried Lydia involuntarily.

Grandpapa, his face tense and his breathing very loud, never looked at her, but both the aunts said, "Hush!"

So she stood quite silent, very much interested and rather frightened, while the tiny, taut old frame twisted itself to the perpendicular, and at last stood erect. Then, and then only, Grandpapa accepted the support of Aunt Beryl's arm to supplement that of the stick as he went very, very slowly downstairs, one step at a time.

Aunt Evelyn, following behind with Lydia, explained to her that Grandpapa never allowed anyone to help him out of his chair.

"You will learn all the little ways of the house in time," said Aunt Evelyn kindly. "You know we hope that this is to be your home."

"Yes, auntie," said Lydia submissively.

A dim, resentful consciousness was slowly creeping over her that "to learn all the little ways of the house" is the endless and often uncongenial concomitant to that orphaned state to which she had proudly laid claim.

II

It was not difficult to learn the routine of life at Regency Terrace. By the end of the autumn Lydia felt as though she had always lived there.

It was very monotonous.

Breakfast was at eight o'clock, and Lydia found herself expected to partake of bread-and-milk, to which she was not accustomed, and which rather annoyed her because she knew they only gave it to her in order to satisfy Grandpapa's old-fashioned sense of the appropriate.

Immediately after breakfast she went out, so as to give Aunt Beryl time to see to the housekeeping before her lessons.

"A good brisk walk up and down the Front," her aunt said encouragingly. "There are never many people there early."

After September, indeed, there were hardly ever any people there at all.

Lydia did not dislike her solitary promenades from one end of the Esplanade to the other, except on the days when there was an east wind, when she hated it.

At first she was allowed to take Grandpapa's dog, Shamrock, with her, although with many misgivings on the part of Aunt Beryl. Shamrock was reputedly a Sealyham terrier, and Grandpapa was inordinately attached to him. He roared with laughter when Uncle George said angrily that the dog made a fool of him by flattening himself under the front wheel of the bicycle which daily conveyed Uncle George to his office; and when Shamrock made all Regency Terrace hideous with howls, on the few occasions that Uncle George kicked him out of the way, Grandpapa's deafness immediately assailed him in its most pronounced form, and he assured his daughter that he could hear nothing at all, and that it was all her fancy.

"Good little dog, Shamrock," said Grandpapa approvingly, when Shamrock prostrated himself in an attitude of maudlin affection before the old man's arm-chair, as he invariably did, to the disgust of the household.

He also showed himself scrupulously obedient to Grandpapa's lightest word, although unfortunate Aunt Beryl might still be hoarse from prolonged cries at the hall-door in a vain endeavour to defend the bare legs of hapless little passing children, whom Shamrock took a delight in terrifying, although he never hurt them.

Lydia liked Shamrock because he always pranced along so gaily, and wagged his tail so effusively, and also because she suspected him of more than sharing her dislike of the parrot.

But their walks together were not a success. There was only one crossing, but Shamrock always contrived to negotiate it as badly as possible under an advancing tram, thus causing the driver to shout angrily at Lydia. He would simulate sudden, delighted recognitions of invalid old ladies in bath-chairs, and hurl himself upon them with extravagant demonstrations, until the bath-chair men, to most of whom he was only too well known, would seize him by the scruff of the neck and hurl him away.

Finally, as he never entered the house when Lydia did, but invariably contrived to give her the slip and extended the excursion by himself, Aunt Beryl no longer allowed her to take him out. Lydia was sorry, but she made no lamentations. If one lived with people, it was always better to conform to their wishes, she had long ago discovered. Her innate philosophy waxed with the disproportionate rapidity sometimes seen in children who are dependent on other than their natural surroundings, for a home.

Crudely put, she conformed to each environment in which she found herself, but—and in this, Lydia, without knowing it, was exceptional—she never lost a particle of her own strong individuality. She merely waited, quite unconsciously, for an opportunity when it might expediently be set free.

With Aunt Beryl she was a docile, rather silent little girl. Aunt Beryl gave her lessons every morning from "Little Arthur", and set her arithmetic problems of which Lydia knew very well that she did not herself know the workings, and to which she merely looked up the answers in a key, and also made her practise scales upon the piano in the drawing-room.

"It will make your fingers nice and supple, even if one or two of the keys won't sound," said Aunt Beryl. "I'll write a note to the piano tuner next week."

But she never did.

Lydia thought gloomily that she was learning even less now than in the old days in London, when her mother had, at least, taught her scraps of French, and given her innumerable books to read. Aunt

17

Beryl declared that Lydia could go on with French by herself, and a French grammar was bought.

"I'll hear you say your verbs," said Aunt Beryl, harassed, "but I've forgotten my accent long ago."

As for books, there were none in the Regency Terrace house. When Aunt Beryl wanted to read, she had recourse to *Weldon's Fashion Journal*, or to an occasional *Home Chat*. Grandpapa had the daily paper read to him, but her aunt once told Lydia that "Grandpapa used to be a great reader, but he can't see now without glasses, and he won't use them. So he never reads."

Uncle George, indeed, often brought home a book from the Public Library in the evenings, but he did not offer to lend them to Lydia, neither did such titles attract her as "Goodman's Applied Mechanics," or somebody else's "Theory of Heat, Light, and Sound". Aunt Beryl, however, was kind, and when Lydia had once said that she liked reading, she promised her a story-book for Christmas. It was then October.

Meanwhile she taught her needlework, and Lydia learnt to make her own blouses, and to knit woollen underwear for a necessitous class vaguely designated by Aunt Beryl as "the pore".

Sewing was the only thing that Aunt Beryl taught Lydia in such a way as to make it interesting. She had no lessons after dinner, which was in the middle of the day. Sometimes in the afternoon she walked slowly on the Esplanade with Aunt Beryl beside Grandpapa's chair, but more often, as the weather grew colder, she and Aunt Beryl went out alone, and then they walked briskly into what Aunt Beryl called "the town". The part where Regency Terrace stood was the "residential quarter".

"The town" mainly consisted of King Street and one of those tributary streets where the shops were. Lydia rather liked the shopping expeditions with Aunt Beryl, and felt important when the grocer's boy or the ironmonger's young lady took an order, and said, "Yes, Miss Raymond. Good afternoon, Miss Raymond," without asking for any address.

Sometimes when Aunt Beryl's list was a long one, and the darkness of approaching winter fell early, she took Lydia in to have tea at a small establishment known to King Street as the "Dorothy Cayfe," and the shopping was resumed afterwards, in the cheerful light of the prevalent gas. This happened seldom, however, as Aunt Beryl liked to be at home, in order to give Grandpapa his tea—which was not wonderful, since whenever she failed to do so her parent never omitted to make caustic allusion to the "long outing that she must have been enjoying in the good fresh air."

When Aunt Beryl had duly been present at the rite of tea, however, it was an understood thing that she went out for a couple of hours afterwards, and left Lydia to entertain Grandpapa. "I am just going to step round to the Jacksons, dear, with my work. I'll be back by six o'clock or so." That was really the time that Lydia liked best.

She soon found out that with Grandpapa she might be her own shrewd, little cynical self. He only required outward decorum and an absence of any modern slang or noisiness, which accorded well with Lydia's natural taste and early training.

She also speedily discovered that Grandpapa thought her clever and that so long as her opinions and judgments were her own, he was ready to listen to them with amusement and interest. Any affectation or insincerity he would pounce upon in a moment. "Don't humbug," he sometimes said sharply. "It's the worst policy in the world. Humbug always ends in muddle."

"Shamrock's a humbug," said the old man once, chuckling as he fondled the little white dog. "He's a humbug and he'll come to a bad end. When I'm dead, they'll get rid of Shamrock. They think I'm taken in by his humbug, but I know he's a bad dog."

Lydia could not help thinking that "they" had some excuse in supposing Grandpapa to be blind and deaf to his protégé's iniquities, but she put out her hand and patted the dog's rough head.

"Would you look after Shamrock, Lyddie?"

"Yes, Grandpapa, I am very fond of him."

"Why?" said Grandpapa sharply.

"Because he amuses me," answered Lydia truthfully.

"Ah ha! we all find it amusing to see other people being made fools of!" was Grandpapa's charitable sentiment. "Well, you shall have him one of these days, Lyddie. I hope you'll have a good home to give him. What do you mean to do when you're grown up?"

"Write books," said Lydia.

To Aunt Beryl she would have said, "Get married and have two boys and a little girl, auntie"—but her Aunt Beryl would never have dreamt of asking her this question.

"Heigh?" said Grandpapa, in a rather astonished voice.

"Write books."

"A blue stocking never gets a husband," said Grandpapa sententiously.

Lydia did not know what a blue stocking was, although she deduced that it was no compliment to be called one, but she was too proud to ask.

"What sort of books do you want to write?"

"Stories," said Lydia, "and perhaps poetry."

"Have you ever tried?"

"Yes, Grandpapa."

"One of these days," said Grandpapa, with cautious vagueness, "you may read me one of your stories, and we shall see what we shall see; but you mustn't expect to make a living by writing books, Lyddie. That's a thing that's only done by hard work."

"What sort of hard work?"

"There's very little hard work that women are fit for. They can go governessing, or school teaching, or nurse in hospitals. Your Aunt Beryl had a fancy that way once, but I told her she'd get as much nursing as she wanted at home, all in good time, and you see I was quite right."

"Did Aunt Evelyn want to do something, too?"

"She wanted to get married, my dear, and so she took the first young fellow that came after her. Never you do that, Lyddie."

Lydia raised surprised eyes to the old man's face.

"Well, well," said Grandpapa soothingly, "you've got twice the brains of any of them, we know that. You get them from your mother. Not that brains ever did her any good, poor soul—she was unbalanced, as clever women generally are."

"Am I unbalanced, Grandpapa?"

"Now that's a bad habit," said Grandpapa, suddenly extending a gnarled forefinger like a little twisted bit of old ivory, as though about to lay it on some objectionable insect. "That's a very bad habit, Lyddie, me dear. Don't refer everything back to yourself. It bores people. Do it in your own mind," said Grandpapa, chuckling; "no doubt you won't be able to help it—but not out loud. When someone tells you that Mrs. Smith dresses better than she walks, don't immediately go and say, like nine women out of every ten, 'Do I dress better than I walk?'"

Grandpapa assumed a piping falsetto designed to simulate a feminine voice: "And don't say, either, 'Oh, that reminds me of what was said about *me* this time nine years ago.' People don't want to hear about you—they want to hear about themselves."

"Always, Grandpapa?" said Lydia, dismayed.

"Practically always, and when you've grasped that, you've got the secret of success. *Always let the other people talk about themselves.*"

Lydia's memory was a retentive one, and to the end of her life, at the oddest, most unexpected moments, Grandpapa's aphorism, delivered in the very tones of his cracked, sardonic old voice, was des-tined to return to her, always with increased appreciation of its cyni-cal penetration into the weakness of human nature:

"*Always let the other people talk about themselves.*"

With the advent of Aunt Beryl and the lamp, needless to say, Grandpapa ceased imparting these educational items to Lydia.

He listened to Aunt Beryl's account of Mrs. Jackson's asthma, agreed that Uncle George was late back from the office, and became deaf and vacant-eyed when Aunt Beryl reproachfully said that Shamrock had brought a live crab into the front hall, and upset the girl's temper. At seven o'clock, Aunt Beryl and Lydia went away to don evening blouses, and, in the case of Aunt Beryl, a "dressy" black silk skirt, and half an hour later they all had supper in the din-ing-room.

Once a week, Wednesdays, Mr. Monteagle Almond, from the Bank, used to come in at nine o'clock and play chess with Uncle George. He told Lydia once that he had never missed a Wednesday evening, except when either or both were away, during the last fif-teen years.

"And I don't suppose," solemnly said Mr. Almond, "I shall miss one for the next fifteen—not if we're both spared."

He was a dried-up-looking little man, with a thin beard and a nearly bald head, and both Uncle George and Aunt Beryl chaffed him facetiously from time to time on the subject of getting married, but Mr. Monteagle Almond never retaliated by turning the tables on them, as Lydia privately considered that he might well have done.

On the evenings when Mr. Almond was not present, Aunt Beryl very often took off her shoes and rested her feet, which were always causing her pain, against the rung of a chair. Sometimes, when Gertrude had cleared away, she hung over the dining-room table, spread with paper patterns and rolls of material, and after hovering undecidedly for a long while, would suddenly pounce on her largest pair of scissors and begin to slash away with every appearance of recklessness. But the recklessness was always justified when the dress or the blouse was finished. She was never too much absorbed to remember Lydia's bedtime, however, and at nine o'clock every night Lydia was expected to rouse Grandpapa from the light slumber into which he would never admit that he had fallen, Uncle George from the newspaper or "Applied Mechanics," and shake hands with them gravely as she said good night.

Only the game of chess might not be interrupted.

Aunt Beryl always came up to say good night to Lydia in her

nice little room at the top of the house.

"Sure you're quite warm enough, dear?"

"Yes, quite, thank you, auntie."

"There's another blanket whenever you want one. You've only to say. Have you said your prayers?"

"Yes."

"And brushed your teeth?"

"Yes, auntie."

"Good night, dearie. Sleep well."

Aunt Beryl tucked her up and kissed her, and sometimes she said: "Sleep on your back and tuck in the clothes, and then the fleas won't bite your toes."

Then she went downstairs again, and Lydia never heard her and Uncle George going up to bed, for Grandpapa always refused to stir before twelve o'clock, and sometimes later, and it was necessary that both of them should wait so as to keep him company and eventually take him up to his room. The only variety in the week was Sunday, and even Sundays had their own routine. A later breakfast and a morning in church were succeeded by a heavy midday meal and a somnolent afternoon for Aunt Beryl and Grandpapa. Uncle George very often took Lydia for a long walk, in the course of which he became more than ever like Mr. Barlow, and would suddenly, while crossing the railway bridge, propound such inquiries as:

"Now, what do you suppose is meant by the word *Tare*, on the left-hand bottom corner of those trucks?"

Lydia very seldom knew the answer to these conundrums, but whether she did or no, she was sufficiently aware that no scientific precision of reply on her part would have given her uncle half the satisfaction that it did to enlighten her ignorance. Accordingly, she generally said demurely:

"I've often wondered, Uncle George. I should like to know what it means."

She always listened to Uncle George's accurate and painstaking explanations and tried to remember them. Suspecting extraordinary deficiencies in Aunt Beryl's system of education, she was genuinely desirous of supplementing them whenever she could.

Her ambitions to acquire learning, accomplishments, and the achievement of extreme personal beauty, all of which seemed to her to be equally far from realization, were Lydia's only troubles at Regency Terrace.

On the former questions she had determined to approach either her uncle or her grandfather after Christmas. Not before, Lydia shrewly decided, or they would say that she was in too great a hurry, that she had not yet had a fair trial of the system of regular lessons at home. In foresight and appraisement of valuation where the touchstone of what she considered to be her own best interest was concerned, Lydia's judgment and calm, unchildlike tenacity of purpose might have been envied by a financier. But to the question of her own appearance, she brought all the ridiculous finality, childish vanity and exaggeration, of twelve-year-old femininity. She spent a long time in front of her small looking-glass, almost every day, staring at her little pointed face, seeking desperately for traces of beauty in her olive skin and straight brows and wishing that her eyes were blue, or brown, or even grey—anything except a dark, variable sort of hazel. The only satisfaction she got was from the contemplation of her hair, which was long and dark and very thick. Aunt Beryl made her wear it in two plaits, during the day-time, but Lydia did not dislike this; as the plaits undone and carefully brushed out in the evenings, gave a momentary wave to the perfectly straight mass.

Lydia brushed it off her forehead and fastened it back with a round comb, and thought that she looked rather like the pictures of "Alice Through the Looking-Glass."

She was tall for her age, which was another source of satisfaction, but the length of her slim hands and feet were a terrible portent of inordinate future growth, and Aunt Beryl, with a foresight unappreciated by her niece, insisted upon a precautionary and unsightly tuck in all Lydia's garments.

But in spite of the tucks, and the frequent east wind, and Aunt Beryl's lessons, and the complete absence of any society of her own age, Lydia liked Regency Terrace very much.

She had an odd appreciation for the security implied by the very monotony of each day as it slipped by. With her mother there had been no security at all. They had come from China when Lydia was five, and she could only just remember a little about the voyage, and the terrible parting from her Amah. After that, they had been in London, sometimes at a boarding-house sometimes in rooms, once in a big hotel where Lydia had had her first alarming, unforgettable experience of going up and downstairs in a lift. When Lydia was six, and her father had gone back to China, she and her mother had stayed first with one relation and then with another, and none of the visits had been very comfortable nor successful. Lydia's mother had cried and said that no one understood the sort of thing she was used to in Hong Kong, and what a dreadful change it was for her to be without a man to look after her.

Lydia, a detached and solemn little girl, had retained from those early years a dislike of scenes and tears, and self-pitying rhapsodies, that was to remain with her for the rest of her life.

They were in London when Lydia's mother became a widow and the next three years had been worse than ever.

Lydia was sent to stay with Aunt Evelyn, and then, just as she was beginning to feel rather more at home with her noisy, teasing cousins, her mother fetched her away again and they went to rooms in Hampstead. But the landlady there objected to the number of times that Lydia's mother asked her friends, although only one at a time, to come and have supper and spend the evening. The two ladies would sit up very late, while Lydia's mother talked of all that made her unhappy, and generally cried a great deal, and very often, even after the visitor had gone, would come and wake Lydia up by kneeling at her bedside and sobbing there.

From Hampstead, her mother went as paying guest to a family in West Kensington and Lydia was sent to a boarding-school. She never forgot the mortification of her mother's sudden descent upon her, when she had been there nearly a whole term, to say that she had come to take her away.

"But she's getting on so well!" the head mistress, whom Lydia liked, had protested. "You're very happy with us, aren't you, dear?"

"Yes," Lydia had muttered miserably, and with only too much truth.

She had been happier than ever before, and had made friends with other little girls, and enjoyed the games they played, and the interesting lessons. And she had felt almost sure of getting a prize at the end of the year. But she knew with a dreadful certainty that if she showed her great reluctance to leaving school, and her disappointment and humiliation at being taken away without rhyme or reason, her mother would have a fit of the tempestuous crying that Lydia so dreaded, and would say how heartless it was of her little girl not to want to come home, "now that they only had each other." So she swallowed very hard, and looked down on the floor, clenching her hands, and made hardly any protest at all. Her only comfort was that her mother's impetuosity, which could never wait, insisted upon her immediate departure. And Lydia was glad to avoid any farewells, with the astonished questions and comments that must have accompanied them.

She felt that she could never bear to see the nice Kensington school again.

After that she had lessons or holidays as seemed good to her mother, and very seldom spent a consecutive three months in the same place. No wonder that Regency Terrace, unaltered in half a century, seemed a very haven of refuge to Mrs. Raymond's child.

III

EXPERIENCE has to be bought, generally at the cost of some humiliating youthful mistakes. Those who profit by these unpleasant transactions early in life may be congratulated.

Lydia, the anxious diplomatist, so acutely desirous of keeping in the good graces of those who had control of her destiny, found that she had made a mistake in approaching Grandpapa privately upon the momentous subject.

Grandpapa, indeed, had received her carefully-thought-out explanation with not too bad a grace.

"So you don't think you're learning enough, eh, Lyddie? D'you think you know more than Aunt Beryl already?"

Lydia had nearly cried.

"No, Grandpapa," she began in the horrified accents of outraged conventionality, when she remembered in time Grandpapa's uncanny faculty for penetrating to one's real true, inmost opinion.

"Not more," she said boldly, "but I know as much of Little Arthur's History as there is in the book, and auntie can't take me any further in French or fractions, and she never has time to give me proper music lessons. I only do scales, and Weber's Last Valse, by myself. And I can *feel* I'm not getting on, Grandpapa—and I do so want to."

"Why?"

"I've got to earn my own living," said Lydia, rather proud of the words, "and besides, I'm going to write books."

"Can you spell?"

"Yes, Grandpapa."

"You'll be the first woman of my acquaintance that could, then," said Grandpapa unbelievingly.

"But there are heaps of other things I ought to know besides spelling," she urged.

"Well, I suppose that's true. But what is it you want to do? I won't pay for a Madame to come and parlyvoo every day," said Grandpapa in sarcastic allusion to a recent flight on the part of Aunt

Beryl's friends, the Jacksons.

"Would it be very expensive to let me go to school for a little bit, Grandpapa?"

"What, and come back a great hulking tomboy, all muddy boots, and scratched hands like your cousins?"

There was less opposition than Lydia had expected in his manner, and she began to plead eagerly.

"I wouldn't, truly I wouldn't—I needn't play games at all. It's only for the lessons I want to go. Beatrice and Olive only like it for the hockey, they *hate* their lessons. But I would work all the time, Grandpapa, and bring back heaps of prizes."

"Mind, if I let you go at all, it would be only as a day boarder," said Grandpapa warningly. But there was more than a hint of concession in his tone.

"That's all I want," said Lydia.

"I'll think it over, and talk to your aunt. Now go and fetch me to-day's paper."

Grandpapa occasionally made a feint of reading the newspaper to himself, although he was never seen to turn over a page.

"I can't, Grandpapa. Aunt Beryl took it away, but she is going to bring it back this evening."

"You *can't*?" said Grandpapa in a voice that contrived to be terrible, although it was so small and high-pitched: "Don't talk nonsense! There's no such thing as *can't*. There's *won't*, if you like."

Lydia felt very much distressed. Grandpapa's anger and contempt were not pleasant at any time, and just now when he appeared so nearly disposed to grant her heart's desire, she was less than ever wishful of incurring them.

"Aunt Beryl has lent the paper to Mrs. Jackson for something," she faltered, feeling much disposed to cry. "She said you were sure not to want it before to-night."

"Quite wrong. I want it at once. Now don't say *can't* again," said Grandpapa sharply.

The unfortunate Lydia looked helplessly at her tyrant.

"There's no such thing as *can't*," said Grandpapa truculently. "Just you take hold of that and don't you ever forget it. Never place any reliance on a person who says *can't*. Let 'em say they won't—or they don't want to—that may be true. The other isn't. Anybody can do anything, if they only make up their minds to it."

Grandpapa and his descendant faced one another in silence for a minute or so across the echo of this Spartan theory. At last the old man said contemptuously:

"If you haven't learnt *that* yet, you're not ready for any more schooling than we can give you here, I can tell you."

It was as Lydia had feared!

The future of one's education, the whole of one's career in fact, was at stake.

Lydia gulped at an enormous lump in her throat and managed to articulate with sufficient determination:

"I'll fetch it."

Then she hurried out of the room, wondering what on earth she should do next.

Rush out and buy another paper?

The shops were a long way off, and very likely the morning papers might be all sold out.

The station book stall?

That again was open to the same objections.

Borrow one from somebody else?

But whom?

Suddenly Lydia caught her breath.

Why not? It seemed obvious, once one had thought of it.

She hastily put on her hat, left the front door ajar behind her, and walked out into the road and down a street that ran at an angle to Regency Terrace.

"If you please, Mr. Raymond would be glad to have the morning paper back again if Mrs. Jackson has quite finished with it," she said politely, relieved that it was late enough in the day for "the girl" to open the door of the Jackson establishment to her, instead of one of the family.

Five minutes later she was again confronting Grandpapa, this time feeling triumphant and highly pleased with herself.

"I've got it, Grandpapa!"

Grandpapa's claw-like old hand shot out and snatched at the newspaper.

"What's the date on it?" he demanded.

Lydia read it aloud.

"That's to-day's all right."

"I went round and asked——" began Lydia, desirous of exploiting her resourcefulness.

"That'll do, me dear. Never spoil an achievement by a long story about it," said Grandpapa. "I asked for the paper and you've brought it. That's quite enough."

"Yes, Grandpapa," said Lydia submissively.

Grandpapa pointed the moral no further but Lydia had unconsciously added another paragraph to the Book of Rules which was to guide her throughout the mysterious game that was just beginning for her: "There's no such thing as can't."

She heard nothing more for the next few days of her ambitious request to be sent to school, and was far too cautious to risk a peremptory refusal through importunity.

It was a week later that she became uncomfortably aware of an indefinable alteration in her aunt's manner towards her.

"Is anything the matter, auntie?" she gently ventured.

"Why should anything be the matter, dear?" said Aunt Beryl, her lips very close together and her gaze not meeting Lydia's.

The child's heart sank.

Quite obviously Aunt Beryl was offended, and meant to adopt the trying policy of ignoring any cause for offence. Twice she was too tired to come upstairs and say good night to Lydia, although this had never happened before, and several times when Lydia made little obvious comments, of the sort that always constituted conversation between them on their walks, Aunt Beryl appeared to be too much absorbed in thought to have heard her.

"I would much rather be scolded," reflected Lydia dismally.

She was not scolded, but Aunt Beryl's sense of grievance presently passed into a more articulate stage.

"Oh, don't ask *me*, dear. I'm nobody. *I* don't know anything," she suddenly exclaimed with extreme bitterness, on a request for advice in respect of Lydia's knitting.

"Oh, auntie! are you angry?"

"Why should I be angry, dear? I may be *grieved*, but that's another matter."

On this ground Aunt Beryl finally took her stand.

"I'm not angry, dear—I'm grieved."

And grieved Aunt Beryl remained, tacitly waving away all Lydia's timid attempts at apology or explanation.

Could anything be better calculated to make one feel thoroughly remorseful and uncomfortable?

Lydia, however, characteristically felt more resentful than remorseful.

The tension of the situation was slightly relieved one evening, greatly to Lydia's surprise, by Mr. Monteagle Almond.

"So you're being sent to school, young lady?" he remarked quietly, making Lydia jump.

"Oh, am I?"

"You ought to know. I understand that a certain young lady, not a hundred miles away from where we are now, asked to be sent to school, so that she might grow very learned. Isn't that so?"

"I *should* like to go to school," faltered Lydia.

"Very natural," said Mr. Almond indulgently. "Companions of your own age attract you, no doubt. What would childhood be without other children, eh, George? You remember?"

"I was not so well provided as you were, Monty," said Uncle George rather resentfully.

"Indeed, no. Are you aware, young lady, that I was one of a family of fifteen?"

Aunt Beryl made a clicking sound with her tongue.

"Yes, Miss Raymond, fifteen. My father and mother were old-fashioned people, and held that each child carried a blessing with it. Three died in infancy, and a young brother was lost at sea. Otherwise I'm thankful to say that we are all spared to this day."

"Fancy!" said Aunt Beryl in a flat voice.

"Fifteen children," repeated the grey-bearded clerk, "and my mother kept her figure to the last day of her life. A lesson to the young wives of to-day, I often think."

"Your bedtime, Lydia," said Aunt Beryl briskly. "Go upstairs now and I'll come and put the light out."

Lydia was much too tactful to point out that it was still ten minutes before her bedtime, understanding perfectly that the indiscreetness of Mr. Monteagle Almond's conversation was responsible for her accelerated departure.

She had learnt that she was really going to school, and she was happy.

Aunt Beryl gradually became reconciled to the loss of her pupil, and presently began to show signs of pride in Lydia's advancement.

Once or twice Lydia heard her talking to Mrs. Jackson in the rapid undertones always adopted by Aunt Beryl and Aunt Evelyn with their friends.

"Quite a backward child, when she came to us last year. Between ourselves, my sister-in-law never took much trouble.... I was quite against sending her to Miss Glover's at first—you know, I thought she'd be so behind in everything. So she was, too, but the way that child has picked up! You really wouldn't believe it—I'm sure half the sums in her book I couldn't do myself. Never was good at figures."

Lydia was very proud of her faculty for arithmetic. She thought very little of being first in her class for English composition, and none of the other girls thought much of it either, but they all envied her when the weekly announcement came, as it frequently did:

"Problem No. 15. No one got that right except Lydia Raymond. Stand up, Lydia Raymond, and show the class the working of No. 15 on the black-board. 'If a train left Glasgow at 8.45 a.m. on Wednesday, travelling at the rate of 60 miles an hour——'"

Lydia enjoyed those problems, worked by herself on the black-board in full view of half-a-dozen befogged, pencil-chewing seniors.

But for her French, Lydia would have found herself more highly placed than she was in the school.

Monday and Thursday afternoons.

O horrible verbs, O hateful *Première Année de Grammaire*, and thrice-hateful genders!

Why should a table be feminine and an arm-chair masculine?

Lydia hated her French, and continued to say "Esker le feneter de la salong ay ouvere?" in a lamentable voice and an unalterably British accent. Very few of Miss Glover's girls were "good at French." Only three had any acquaintance with German, and of these one was Dutch.

Many of them could play the piano correctly, and even brilliantly, some of them could copy free-hand drawings or plaster casts, but hardly one could write a letter without making mistakes in spelling, punctuation, and English. All, unconsciously enough, were more or less defective in the correct pronunciation of English.

Since brains, in Great Britain, are for the most part the prerogative of the middle classes, it follows that their possessors enjoy a certain prestige among their compeers which would, on those same grounds, be denied them in more exalted circles.

Lydia found that her schoolfellows were proud of her cleverness, and disposed to seek her friendship.

She easily assumed leadership amongst the group of girls of her own age who were also day boarders at Miss Glover's.

"*Do* help me with this beastly sum, Lydia. I'm sure you can do it."

Lydia always acceded very graciously to such frequent requests, partly because she loved to show her own superior attainments, and partly because of a very definite conviction, which she had never yet put into words, that it was always worth while to show oneself agreeable. In consequence of this complacence, she was seldom at a loss for companionship in play-time. There was always someone to walk about with, arms round one another's waists after the immemorial schoolgirl practice, heads close together under black or scarlet tam o' shanter, for a better exchange of confidences.

Then Lydia put into practice Grandpapa's Golden Rule: *Always let the other people talk about themselves.*

"I say, Lydia, I'll tell you a secret. Mind, now, you're not to say a word to anyone, because I promised not to tell ... but I know I can trust you?"

An interrogative turn to that last sentence.

"Yes, truly you can, Ethel. Tell me."

"Well, promise you won't tell. Not even if you're asked?"

"Cross my heart——" in the glib, accustomed formula.

"Well, then, Daisy Butcher and May Holt have had a row. You know what *frightful* friends they've been ever since the beginning of the term? Well, it's all over, and they've quarrelled. Only don't ever say I said so because Edith told me, and I said I wouldn't say because it was May Holt herself who told her, and she made her promise not to say. I wouldn't say a word myself, only I really thought you *ought* to know, sitting next to May in class and everything. I say, do you *like* May Holt?"

Lydia, who thought May Holt common and stupid, was for a moment tempted to say so. Then, innate caution and a distrust of her companion's garrulity restrained her.

"She's all right," she said vaguely. "I thought you were rather friends with her?"

"Not now," said Ethel hastily. "If the quarrel comes out and there's any taking sides, I shall be on Daisy's side. I think May Holt's been awfully mean. I simply can't bear mean ways. I'm like that, you know."

Thus Ethel's confidences, similar to scores of others, all ending in an exposition of the speaker's view of her own personal traits of character.

Storms raged in teacups, confidences were violated, the identical Ethel who had sworn Lydia to secrecy on the May and Daisy quarrel, found herself taxed with various indiscreet utterances and sent to Coventry.

"Well, it was Edith who told me, and she said May Holt was a liar, what's more," sobbed Ethel, in counter-accusation that availed her nothing, although it raised fresh and terrible issues between herself and Edith, and again between Edith and May Holt, and all May Holt's partisans.

Lydia listened to it all, and thought how clever she had been to keep clear of all this trouble.

It was a thing always to be remembered—the unwisdom of uttering opinions that would probably be repeated to their object—never,

never to say anything that could not be safely repeated without making for one an enemy.

Lydia silently added this conviction to her increasing store of worldly wisdom.

So she welcomed the confidences of the other girls, most of whom seemed quite unable to prevent themselves from talking, and she was at the same time very careful never to render herself unpopular by mischief-making or by carrying backwards and forwards any of their indiscreet utterances.

"You can always trust Lydia," said one or two of the girls.

And once she heard one of them exclaim:

"I've never heard Lydia Raymond say an unkind word about anybody."

It sounded very sweet and charitable, but Lydia, with a sense of humour not unlike her grandfather's, had a little grim, private laugh at the irony of it.

Several of her schoolfellows asked her to tea, or to an occasional picnic in the summer, but Lydia very often regretfully said that her aunt did not like her to go out much, and declined the invitations, without ever referring them to Aunt Beryl at all.

She had a fastidious idea that she did not want to be reputed "great friends" with the children of the more superior tradespeople, or even with the two youthful social lights of the establishment, the daughters of a rich local dentist.

Instinct, and certain recollections of her mother, led her to seek the friendship of a quiet little girl, actually a boarder, whose home was in the west of England, and of whom Lydia only knew that her father was a clergyman, and that she had nice manners and somehow spoke differently from the others. Her name was Nathalie Palmer.

Nathalie did not make so many confidences as did the other girls, and when she did talk to Lydia it was of Devonshire and of her own home, not of the people at school.

This Lydia observed, instinctively approved, and inwardly made note of for future imitation.

As Nathalie knew no one outside the school, she was naturally unable to ask Lydia to come home with her, but just before the midsummer break-up her father came to visit her.

He stayed for two days at the Seaview Hotel, and Nathalie took Lydia to luncheon there.

Mr. Palmer looked old to be the father of fourteen-year-old Nathalie, and had a slow, clerical manner of speech that rather overawed Lydia.

She had never had a meal at any hotel since the days with her mother and father in London, that seemed now so immeasurably remote, and she felt rather nervous. Politely answering Mr. Palmer's kind inquiries as to her place in class, her favourite games and lessons, she was all the time anxiously casting surreptitious glances at Nathalie to see how she helped herself to the strange and numerous dishes proffered by the waiter.

Aunt Beryl was very particular about "table-manners," but at Regency Terrace there was never any such bewildering profusion of knives and forks to perplex one.

Once Lydia embarked upon the butter-dish, offered by Mr. Palmer, with her own small knife, and then, leaving it in the butter-dish, found only a very large knife left beside her plate with which to spread it.

Shame and disaster threatened.

Lydia looked up, and her distressed gaze met that of a waiter. To her own effable surprise, she made a movement of her head that brought him deferentially to her elbow with the required implement. Simplicity itself!

Lydia inwardly decided that one need never be frightened, in the most unaccustomed surroundings, if only one kept one's head and never betrayed any sense of insecurity.

Next day she had the gratification of being shyly told by Nathalie:

"Father said what a pretty face you had, Lydia, and what nice manners. He was so glad I'd got such a nice friend, and he said I might ask you whether one day your aunt would let you come and stay with us during the holidays."

IV

WHEN Lydia was fifteen, expectant of Honours in her examinations, highly placed in the school, and with a secret hope that the following term might see her Head of the School—and that, moreover, at an unprecedently early age—unexpected disaster overtook her.

The three placid years at Regency Terrace had been so little marked by any changes that she had forgotten that old sense of the insecurity and impermanence of life, bred of early days with her mother, and it came as a shock to her that anything should interfere seriously with her schemes.

Quite unexpectedly she fell ill.

"I don't like that cough of yours, Lydia."

"It's only a cold, auntie."

"It doesn't seem to get any better. Let me see, how long have you had it now?"

Lydia pretended to think that Aunt Beryl was only talking to herself, and bent lower over her books. She always worked at her preparation in the evenings after supper now.

It was damp, chilly weather, and her cough grew worse, although she stifled it as far as possible, and said nothing about the pains in her back and sides.

Aunt Beryl brought her a bottle of cough mixture recommended by Mrs. Jackson, and Lydia put it on the mantelpiece in her bedroom, and carefully dusted the bottle every day, and sometimes poured away a little of the contents.

But one morning, one important morning when there was a French lesson which it was essential that Lydia, with whom French still remained the weakest of links in an otherwise well-forged chain, should attend, she found herself quite unable to go downstairs to breakfast.

Her head swam, her eyes and mouth were burning, and her legs unaccountably trembled beneath her.

"No such thing as *can't*," muttered Lydia fiercely, repeating Grandpapa's favourite axiom.

The pain in her side had increased without warning, and suddenly gave her an unendurable stab every time that she tried to move.

"*Oh!*"

Lydia sank back on the bed, and found herself crying hoarsely from pain and dismay. Surely even Grandpapa would admit the necessity for saying "can't" at last.

But Lydia did not see Grandpapa for some time after that morning.

She lay in bed with a fire in the room, sometimes suffering a great deal of pain, and sometimes in a sort of strange, jumbled dream, when the pattern of the wall paper turned into mysterious columns of figures that would never add up, and French Irregular Verbs danced across the ceiling.

Aunt Beryl nursed her all day and sat up with her at nights very often, and Dr. Young came to see her every day.

Once he said to her:

"You're a very good patient. I don't know what we should have done with you if you hadn't been a good, reasonable girl, and done everything you were told."

Lydia was pleased.

"Am I very ill?" she asked.

"Oh, you've turned the corner nicely now," said Dr. Young cheerfully. "But pneumonia's no joke, and you'll have to be careful for a long while yet."

"Shan't I be able to go up for the examination?"

"Let me see—that's about a month off. We shall have to see about that."

Dr. Young's daughter was at Miss Glover's school, too, and he knew all about the terrible importance of the examination. Nevertheless, he gave Lydia no permission to resume her studies.

"Don't worry, dear, there's plenty of time before you, and now I've got some nice fruit jelly for you," said Aunt Beryl, and Lydia always thanked her very gratefully and lay back against the pillow, trying all the time to recapitulate the French verbs and the list of Exceptions to Rules that she had been learning when she first fell ill.

Except for anxiety about the examination, convalescence was agreeable.

Uncle George came up to see her one day, and brought her some grapes, and explained to her why it was that the great pieces of ice in her glass of barley-water did not cause it to overflow, quite in the old Mr. Barlow manner, and once Nathalie Palmer came by invitation and had tea with her upstairs, and told her how sorry all the girls had been about her illness.

"And you'll miss the exam," moaned Nathalie, "and it seems such a shame. I know you'd have done splendidly."

"What have you been having in class?" asked Lydia.

"Almost all recapitulation. The only really new thing that we're doing is *Henry V.* for literature."

That evening Lydia made Gertrude, the servant, bring her the volume of Shakespeare from the drawing-room.

Her brain felt quite clear now, and her eyes no longer hurt her when she tried to read.

Next day she was allowed to go downstairs for tea.

Aunt Beryl, who looked very tired and sallow, helped her to dress, and Uncle George came upstairs to fetch her, and they both supported her very carefully down the stairs and into the drawing-room, where a fire had been lit, and a special tea laid on a little table beside the arm-chair.

Grandpapa, with Shamrock prancing unrestainedly at his feet, and the parrot, brought up from the dining-room, hanging upside down in his cage on the centre-table, were all waiting to welcome her.

"Very glad to see you down, me dear," said Grandpapa, shaking hands with her formally. "A nasty time you've had, a very nasty time, I'm afraid."

"She's been such a good girl, Grandpapa," said Aunt Beryl, raising her voice as though by a great effort. "Dr. Young says she's the best patient he's ever had."

"Did you have to swallow a great deal of physic, Lyddie? Ah, a very disagreeable thing, physic," said Grandpapa, who was ordered a certain draught daily, which he was only too apt to pour away into the nearest receptacle in the face of all Aunt Beryl's protests.

"Mr. Almond asked after you on Wednesday, Lydia. He has been quite concerned over your illness," Uncle George told her.

Lydia sat back in the arm-chair, her long plaits falling over either shoulder, and could not help feeling that all this attention was rather agreeable.

Aunt Beryl's friend, Mrs. Jackson, "stepped in," to ask how she felt, and to borrow a paper pattern for a blouse, and said she had also heard from Dr. Young and other sources what a good patient Lydia had been.

"And so hard on you, poor child, missing your examinations and all."

"Perhaps Dr. Young will let me go," said Lydia wistfully: "It's only four days, and not till next week."

Mrs. Jackson shook her head doubtfully.

"The Town Hall is well warmed, with those pipes and all, but I don't know. Perhaps if you could go in a closed cab, well wrapped up.... But you've missed such a lot of study, haven't you?"

"I know," said Lydia dejectedly.

They were all very kind to her, and seemed to realize the great disappointment of failing after all, or even of putting off the examination for another year, when one would be nearly sixteen, and no longer the youngest candidate of all.

Mrs. Jackson refused tea, and hurried away with her paper pattern, Shamrock flying to the head of the stairs after her, and breaking into a storm of howls, as though in protest at her departure. Aunt Beryl hastened distressfully after him.

"Hark at that!" said she unnecessarily.

Grandpapa put on his deafest expression.

"This is very trying for you, Lydia," said Uncle George pointedly. "It seems to go through and through one's head."

Did Grandpapa actually throw a glance of concern at the invalid? She could hardly believe her eyes, and felt more than ever how pleasant it was to be the centre of attention.

And then Aunt Beryl came in again, dropped into a chair near the door, oddly out of breath, and quietly fainted away.

Gertrude had been sent for Dr. Young before they could bring her back to consciousness again, and when he did arrive, he and Uncle George almost carried Aunt Beryl up to her room.

"Thoroughly overdone," said Dr. Young. "Miss Raymond has been so very unsparing of herself during her niece's illness—one of those unselfish people, you know, who never think anything about themselves. I am ashamed of myself for not seeing how near she was to a break-down."

Decidedly Aunt Beryl was the heroine of the hour.

Lydia was ashamed of herself for the resentment that this turning of the tables awoke in her.

She went to her own room, unescorted, when the commotion had subsided, and her supper was brought up to her by Gertrude nearly an hour late.

"How is Aunt Beryl now?" she asked.

"Gone to sleep, miss. She is wore out, after sitting up at night, and then the nursing during the day, and seeing to the house and the old gentleman, all just the same as usual—and no wonder."

No wonder, indeed! Everyone said the same.

During the two days that Aunt Beryl, by the doctor's orders, remained upstairs, the household in Regency Terrace had time to realize what, in fact, was the case—that never before had Miss Raymond been absent from her post for more than a few hours at a time.

When Mr. Monteagle Almond came in on Wednesday evening, full of inquiries and congratulations for Lydia, he was hardly allowed time to formulate them.

"It's my poor sister we are anxious about," said Uncle George, just as though Lydia had never been ill at all.

"Quite knocked up with nursing," said Grandpapa, shaking his head. "I've never known Beryl take to her bed before, and we miss her sadly downstairs."

Mr. Monteagle Almond was deeply concerned.

"Dear me, dear me. This is very distressing news. I had no idea of this. Miss Raymond never complains."

"That's it," agreed Uncle George gloomily. "One somehow never thought of her overdoing it."

"Unselfish," said Mr. Almond, adding thoughtfully: "Well, well, well, selfish people have the best of it in this world, there's no doubt."

The little bank clerk was generalizing, according to his fashion, but Lydia felt angry and uncomfortable, as though the reference might have application to herself.

Aunt Beryl certainly looked much as usual when she reappeared downstairs, but it was very evident that two days without her had thoroughly awakened both Grandpapa and Uncle George to a new sense of her importance.

"We must try and spare your aunt as much as possible," Uncle George said gravely to Lydia. "I'm afraid that we've all been allowing her to do far too much for us."

Lydia found it curiously disagreeable to see the focus of general interest thus shifted. Unconsciously, she had occupied the centre place in the little group in Regency Terrace ever since her arrival there, as the twelve-year-old orphan, in her pathetic black frock. Without consciously posing, she had certainly, as the eager student at Miss Glover's bringing back prizes and commendations, been the most striking personality of that small world, and she had known that her elders discussed her cleverness, her steady industry, even her increasing prettiness, as topics of paramount interest.

Lydia, in other words, was complacently aware of being the heroine of that story, which is the aspect worn by life to the imaginative. Now it appeared that this rôle had been summarily usurped by Aunt Beryl.

Lydia's sense of drama was far too keen for her to undervalue the possibilities of the aspect presented by her aunt. It *was* pathetic to have toiled, without appreciation, all these years, to have nursed one's niece devotedly day and night, and then to faint away helplessly without a word of complaint. But the more Lydia realized how pathetic it was, the more annoyed she became.

Her own convalescence was a very rapid one, partly owing to her determination to get to the Town Hall for the examination. Both Grandpapa and Uncle George, with the masculine inability to entertain more than one anxiety at a time, appeared to have forgotten that she had ever been ill, and Dr. Young himself, when applied to, only said:

"Well, well, if you've really set your mind on it—the weather's nice and warm. But you must wrap up well and keep out of draughts. We don't want a relapse, mind. Miss Raymond can't do any more nursing, you know. She ought to be nursed herself."

Lydia would cheerfully have nursed Aunt Beryl, if only to retain her own sense of self-importance, but well did she know that her aunt would give her no such opportunity. Really, unselfish people could be very trying.

She went to the Town Hall, and was greatly restored by the enthusiastic greetings of her fellow-candidates.

"Oh, Lydia, how plucky of you to try, after all! Don't you feel *fearfully* behindhand? Fancy, if you do get through! It'll be even more splendid than if you hadn't been ill, and had no disadvantage of missing such a lot."

Lydia had a shrewd suspicion that she had not missed nearly so much as they all thought. Nathalie had said that most of the work done in class during her absence had been recapitulation, and recapitulation, to Lydia's sound memory and habits of accuracy inculcated by Uncle George, had never been more than a pleasant form of making assurance doubly sure.

For the last two days she had been studying frantically, and had made Nathalie go through *Henry V.* with her, and mark the passages to be learnt by heart.

Fortune favoured her in causing the English Literature paper to be set for the last day of the examination.

When that last day came Lydia felt tolerably certain that she had thoroughly overtaxed her barely-restored strength, and would shortly suffer for it with some severity, but her examination-papers had been a series of inward triumphs.

French had certainly presented its usual stumbling-blocks, but Lydia reasonably told herself that she would probably have experienced at least equivalent difficulties, had she attended every class, and where mechanical rote-learning could avail her, she knew that she was safe. Moreover, the algebra and arithmetic papers, over which most of the candidates were groaning, she could view with peculiar complacency.

"How did you get on?" several of the girls asked her eagerly.

"Not *too* badly, I hope," said Lydia guardedly.

It would be far more of a triumph, if she did succeed, for her success to come as a surprise to everyone. They could hardly expect it, after such an absence from class as hers had been.

Even the governess in charge of the group of girls said to her kindly:

"You mustn't be disappointed if you don't get through this time, dear. Miss Glover knows you've worked very well, and that it's only illness that's thrown you back."

Lydia returned to Regency Terrace thoroughly exhausted.

"I'm sure you've done your best, dear, and if it isn't this time, it'll be next," said Aunt Beryl philosophically. "Now go straight upstairs and have a good rest."

Lydia went, and was not at all displeased to find that her head was throbbing and her face colourless.

The following day the doctor saw her, and shook his head at her.

"Better give her a change of air, Miss Raymond. If you won't go away yourself, it will, anyway, set you rather more free not to have Miss Lydia on your mind."

Lydia felt that the advice might have been worded in a manner more flattering to herself, but she was pleased at the idea of a change.

She had not been away since her first arrival as an inmate of Grandpapa's household. Aunt Beryl's theory was that one went away *to* the sea, not *from* it. If one happened to live by the sea, there was no need to go away at all. Only Uncle George, taking his fortnightly holiday in the summer, departed on a walking or bicycling tour with some bachelor friend of his own.

"You'll enjoy staying with your Aunt Evelyn," said Aunt Beryl. "The girls must be nearly grown up now, I declare. How time flies! Beatrice must be all of eighteen, and Olive sixteen, and I suppose Bob is somewhere between the two of them. How long is it since you've seen them, Lydia?"

"Not since I was quite little—about ten, I think."

"It'll be nice for you to make friends with the girls. I've often wished you had a sister."

Lydia did not echo the wish when she had seen the Senthoven family circle.

"There's no nonsense about *us*," might have been taken for their motto, or even their war-cry.

On the evening of Lydia's arrival she was mysteriously taken possession of by Olive, her youngest cousin, under pretext of unpacking.

"I say, Lydia."

"Yes?"

"*Yes?*" mimicked Olive, with a screwed-up mouth and mincing pronunciation, in derisive mockery of Lydia's low, clear enunciation, which was in part natural, and in part learnt from Nathalie Palmer.

"I declare you're afraid of the sound of your own voice. You ought to hear *us*! My word! we'll make you open your eyes—*and* ears too—before we've done with you. You should just hear the ragging that goes on whenever Bob's at home. Look here, this is what I want to know."

This time Lydia only looked interrogation. She despised Olive too thoroughly to care whether she laughed at her way of speaking or not, but she thought that the sooner Olive satisfied her curiosity and went away the better.

"Do you like *fun*?" said Miss Senthoven, bringing her prominent brown eyes and head of untidy, flopping hair close to Lydia's face in her extreme eagerness for a reply.

Lydia, when she had recovered from her surprise at the form of the inquiry, assented, since assent was obviously expected of her, but she had grave doubts as to whether her own definition of "fun" would coincide with that of the Senthovens.

It did not.

"Fun" was synonymous with noise, and the most brilliant repartee known to any Senthoven was Bob's favourite form of squashing such "nonsense" as a comment on the blueness of the sky: "Well, you didn't expect to see it red, did you?"

Bob, a hobble-de-hoy of seventeen, short and thick-set, was his mother's idol. But there was "no nonsense" allowed from poor Aunt Evelyn by her terrible daughters.

"The mater's so mushy," they shouted disgustedly, when she made excuse, on the morning after Lydia's arrival, for Bob's very tardy appearance.

Lydia looked round the breakfast-table. She was quite well again now, and breakfast upstairs would have been unheard of. Beatrice was a still larger, taller, more athletic, and, if possible, noisier edition of Olive. She had just left school, and her dark hair, very thick and heavy, was piled into untidy heaps at the back of her head.

"No nonsense about *my* hair, I can tell you. Half the time I don't even look in the glass to see how I've done it," Beatrice would declare proudly.

The girls wore flannel shirts, with collars and ties, and short skirts that invariably contrived to be rather longer at the back than they were in the front.

They strenuously refused to make any change of toilette in the evenings, only substituting heelless strapped black shoes for their large and sturdy boots, over their thick-ribbed stockings.

Those evenings were the noisiest that Lydia had ever known.

Only Uncle Robert, small, and sallow, and spectacled, was silent.

He sat at the foot of the table, said a brief, muttered grace, and dispensed the soup.

"I say, what tommy-rot it is your not playing hockey, Lydie. Bee and I have got a match on to-morrow afternoon."

"Can't I come and watch you play?"

"I suppose so. *I* don't care if you do, I'm sure," Olive hastily repudiated the mere suggestion of such a dangerous approach to "nonsense" as was implied by a possible interest in another's movements.

"I say, I do believe Bob gets later every blessed day. A nice row there'd be if *we* came in late for every meal!"

"Too bally hungry to do that!"

"Your brother doesn't get much fresh air. You must remember he's in an office all day, and has two stuffy train journeys, poor boy," said Bob's mother unwisely.

"*Ow!* poor 'ickle sing, then—mammy's own baby-boy!" yelled Beatrice derisively.

"Mater!" said Olive, "how *can* you be so sloppy?"

Lydia looked round her, amazed. No one seemed to think, however, that Beatrice and Olive were behaving otherwise than well and dutiful.

"Beef, Lydia?"

"Yes, please, Uncle Robert."

Lydia saw Beatrice wink at Olive, and Olive stuff a corner of her Japanese paper napkin into her mouth, as though to prevent an explosion of laughter. She only perceived that the jest lay in the manner of her own reply, when to the same inquiry her cousins successively answered, very loudly and curtly.

"Ra-*ther*!"

After the beef Aunt Evelyn helped the pudding. There were two dishes in front of her, one containing the remaining half of the pink mould that had figured on the dinner-table in the middle of the day, and the other the cold remnants of the previous night's tart.

And Lydia, invited to make her choice, replied very clearly and rather defiantly:

"I should like some tart, if you please, Aunt Evelyn."

Bob, who had made his entry with the second course, roared with laughter, and, reaching across his sister Beatrice, banged Lydia heavily on the back.

"That's right, Lady Clara Vere de Vere. You stick to it!"

Lydia, who hated being touched, jumped in her place, but she had the wit to guess that the surest way of making her cousins pursue any particular course of action would be to show that she disliked it, in which case they would instantly look upon her as "fair game." She did not in the least mind the series of witticisms, lasting the length of her visit, designed to emphasize what the Senthovens considered the affectations of her speech.

"Just the weeniest little tiny bit, if you will be so awf'ly kind, please. Thank you so awf'ly much."

Thus Beatrice, humorously.

And Bob:

"Well, perhaps—if you were to press me to a jelly——"

Lydia was not in the least amused at these sallies, but she laughed at them cheerfully enough. She felt immeasurably superior to the Senthovens, and had every intention of proving that superiority to them before the end of her stay.

At first blush, this did not appear to be any too easy. There was no doubt that the Senthovens, the girls especially, were efficient in their own line of action.

Beatrice was a renowned hockey captain; Olive had silver trophies from both the Golf Club and the Swimming Club, and both had won Junior Championships at lawn-tennis.

"Are you a good walker, old girl?" Beatrice one day inquired of Lydia.

This last term of endearment was a sign of the highest goodwill, and if employed too frequently would almost certainly lead to the accusation of sloppiness.

"Oh, yes," said Lydia, thinking of the school crocodile wending its decorous way the length of the Parade.

"Good. Olive's an awful rotter at walking. You and I can do some tramps together. Are you game for a six o'clock start to-morrow morning?"

Lydia laughed, really supposing the suggestion to be humorously intended.

"What are you cackling about? You're such an extraordinary kid; you always seem to laugh with your mouth shut. I suppose they taught you that at this precious school of yours, where you don't even play hockey. Well, what about to-morrow? We can take some sort of fodder with us, but I've got to be back at the Common at ten sharp for a hockey practice."

Lydia was obliged to resign her pretensions. She hadn't understood quite what Beatrice meant by a "good walker."

"Anything up to twenty-five miles is my mark," said Beatrice complacently.

She and Olive were both good-humouredly contemptuous of Lydia's incapabilities, and Bob was even ready to show her how to serve at tennis, and how to throw a ball straight. Lydia was willing to be taught, and was sufficiently conscious that her tennis was improving rapidly, to submit to a good deal of shouting and slangy, good-humoured abuse.

She did not like it, but was philosophically aware that her stay at Wimbledon was drawing to a close, and that she would reap the benefit of improved tennis for ever afterwards.

"I suppose, being a duffer at games, that you're a regular Smart Aleck at lessons, aren't you?" Olive amiably asked her.

An assent would certainly be regarded as "bucking," but, on the other hand, Lydia had no mind to let her claims to distinction be passed over.

"I've just been in for an examination," she said boldly. "I might hear the result any day now."

"Get on! I thought you'd been ill."

"I've missed half the term at school, but I studied by myself, and I was up in time to go to the Town Hall for the exam. I had to go to bed again afterwards, though."

"Do you suppose you've got an earthly?" said Beatrice, in highly sceptical accents.

"Oh, I don't know. You see, I was the youngest competitor of all, as it happened."

Lydia had been very anxious to introduce this last piece of information, and it was plain that Beatrice and Olive were not altogether unimpressed by it.

Aunt Beryl had promised Lydia a telegram as soon as the results of the examination were put up in the Town Hall, and Lydia had already decided that in the event of failure, she should say nothing at all to the Senthovens. They would never remember to ask her about it. But if she had passed, she told herself grimly, they would have to acknowledge that they were not the only people who could succeed. Lydia reflected that she was sick of hearing how Olive had just saved a goal, and Beatrice had conducted her team to victory in yet another hockey match.

V

THE last of Lydia's Saturday afternoons at Wimbledon, however, was at length at hand.

"We might go and have some sort of a rag on the Common to-morrow for Lydia's last day. Sunday doesn't count," said Beatrice, on Friday evening after supper.

"Quite a good egg," agreed Olive. "Bob, are you game?"

Bob assented without enthusiasm. He was stretched at full length on the sofa, with his arms crossed underneath his head.

Uncle Robert was behind his newspaper as usual, and Aunt Evelyn was earnestly perusing a ladies' paper, from which she occasionally imparted to Lydia—the only person who made any pretence at listening to her—certain small items of information regarding personalities equally unknown to both of them.

This was Mrs. Senthoven's one relaxation, and afforded her an evident satisfaction.

"Fancy! It says here that, 'It is rumoured that a certain demoiselle of no inconsiderable charm, and well known to Society, is shortly to exchange her rank as peer's daughter for one even more exalted.' I wouldn't be surprised if that was Lady Rosalind Kelly that was meant. I suppose she's going to marry some duke. They say she's lovely, but I wouldn't care to see a son of *mine* marry her, after all the stories one's heard."

Aunt Evelyn looked fondly at the recumbent Bob.

"I say, we might get the Swaines to come with us to-morrow," said Olive, "then we could get up a rag of some sort."

"I say, old girl, chuck me my pipe. The mater won't mind."

"Get it yourself," retorted Olive, utterly without malice, but in the accepted Senthoven method of repudiating a request for any small service.

"Here's rather a good story about that fellow—you remember, Lydia, we saw his picture in the Sunday paper—Gerald Fitzgerald, who's acting in some play or other. Listen to this!"

Aunt Evelyn read aloud a reputed *mot* of the famous comedian that did not err upon the side of originality.

"I wonder if that's true, now!"

"Bee, chuck me my pipe," from Bob.

No Senthoven ever listened to any piece of information not directly bearing upon their own immediate personal interests.

"No fear! What a slacker you are, Bob! Why don't you get up off that sofa? Lydia's shocked at your ways."

"She's not!"

"She is!"

Lydia hoped that she showed her sense of superiority by contributing nothing to the discussion, which continued upon the simple lines of flat assertion and contradiction until Bob flung a cushion at his sister's head.

Beatrice thereupon hurled herself on him with a sort of howl.

"Don't make so much noise; you'll disturb father. Bee, you really are too old to romp so—your hair is nearly coming down."

It came quite down before Beatrice had finished pommelling her brother, and Uncle Robert had waked, and said that it was too bad that a man who'd been working hard all the week couldn't read the paper in peace and quiet for five minutes in his own house without being disturbed by all this horse-play.

Lydia watched her cousins, despised them very thoroughly indeed, and was more gratified than humiliated when Olive remarked:

"It's easy to see you've never been one of a large family, Lydia. You don't seem to understand what rotting means."

"I wonder you haven't got used to being chaffed at your school. It must be a sloppy sort of place."

"I daresay you'd think so," said Lydia calmly. "But then, you see, the girls there go in for work, not play."

"Oh, they go in for work, not play, do they?" mimicked Olive, but without much spirit, and as though conscious of her extreme poverty of repartee.

Lydia noticed, however, that both the Senthoven girls asked her frequent questions about her school, questions which she answered with all the assurance that she could muster.

That was something else to be remembered: it was better to assume that if your standards differ from those of your surroundings, it is by reason of their superiority.

Lydia lived up to her self-evolved philosophy gallantly, but she was in a minority, against a large majority that had, moreover, the advantage, incalculable in the period of adolescence, of a year or two's seniority.

She did not like the feeling of inferiority, painfully new to her.

At Regency Terrace she was the subject of ill-concealed pride. Even Grandpapa, although he never praised, found no fault with her manners and bearing, and had lately admitted—no small compliment—that "Lyddie could manage Shamrock."

Uncle George discussed chemistry and botany with her seriously, and even allowed her opinion to carry weight in certain small questions of science, and Mr. Monteagle Almond always treated her like a grown person, and alluded respectfully to the rarity of finding a mathematical mind in a woman.

As to Aunt Beryl, in spite of the way in which she had lately usurped Lydia's recent rôle of invalid and acknowledged centre of general interest, Lydia knew very well that her own achievements and capabilities formed the chief theme of Aunt Beryl's every discourse with her friends. At school she was not only liked by her companions, but looked upon as the intellectual pride of the establishment.

No one at Miss Glover's bothered much about games, and, anyhow, Lydia's play at tennis was accounted amongst the best in the school.

It annoyed her to realize, as she most thoroughly did realize, that judged by the Senthoven standards, that best was very mediocre indeed.

She had never played golf, or hockey, or cricket, and her swimming consisted of slow and laborious strokes that grew very feeble, and came at very short intervals if she attempted to exceed a length of fifty yards.

Lydia's ambitions would never be athletic ones, and although she wished to be seen to advantage, she was far too shrewd to attempt any emulation of Beatrice and Olive and their friends upon their own ground. She only wished—and it seemed to her a highly reasonable wish—to show them that, in other and greater issues, she, too, could count her triumphs.

She waited her opportunity with concealed annoyance at its tardiness in coming.

The Saturday afternoon picnic, ostensibly arranged in her honour, was such a form of entertainment as was least calculated to make Lydia enjoy herself.

It began with a noisy *rendezvous* between the Senthoven family and a tribe of male and female Swaines, ranging from all ages between eight and eighteen years old.

Most of the Swaines bestrode bicycles, upon which they balanced themselves whilst almost stationary with astonishing skill, and presently, amid many screams, a female Swaine took Olive and a picnic basket on the step of her machine, and departed with them in the direction of the Common. Bob and three junior Swaine brethren, also on bicycles, laid arms across one another's shoulders, and thus, taking up the whole width of the road, boldly invaded the tram lines, and Beatrice, with her contemporary Swaine and Lydia, started out on foot at a swinging pace.

"Give me *ekker*," said Beatrice contemptuously. "There's no ekker in biking that I can see."

Exercise, Lydia grimly reflected, they were certainly having in abundance. She and Beatrice held either handle of the large picnic hamper containing the Senthovens' contribution to the entertainment, and as it swung and rattled between them, Lydia made increased efforts to accommodate her steps to Beatrice's unfaltering stride.

"I s'pose," presently remarked Beatrice, with that aggressive accent that to a Senthoven merely represented the absence of affectation, "you'll be saying presently that we've walked you off your legs. I never knew such a kid! Here, slack off a bit, Dot—she can't keep up."

"I can," said Lydia.

She had no breath left with which to make a long speech.

Both the elder girls burst out laughing.

"Come on then."

It was a scarlet-faced Lydia, with labouring chest, that eventually dropped on to the selected spot of Wimbledon Common, but she at least had the satisfaction of hearing her own name given in reply to Bob's derisive inquiry as to which of them had set the pace.

Yet another proof of the profound wisdom of Grandpapa who had said, "There's no such thing as *can't*."

Grandpapa's theory, however, was less well exemplified in the impromptu cricket match that presently sprang up, in the sort of inevitable way in which a game that comprised the use of muscles and a ball invariably did spring up whenever the Senthovens were gathered together.

"I don't play cricket," Lydia haughtily observed to the least muscular-looking of the Swaine girls.

"Why not?" said her contemporary, looking very much astonished.

There was nothing for it but to put into words the humiliating admission:

"I don't know how to."

"How funny! But we'll soon teach you."

Lydia resigned herself, and since she was no more deficient in physical courage than is any other imaginative egotist, who sets the importance of cutting a figure far above any incidental bodily risk that may be incurred in cutting in, she successfully avoided at least the appearance of running away from the ball.

The game, of course, was what was known to the Senthovens as "a rag" only, since with deficient numbers and a lack of implements, nothing so serious as a match could be contemplated. Consequently, Lydia presently found herself with Bob's cricket bat tightly grasped in her unaccustomed hands.

She was not altogether displeased. It was only Olive who was bowling, and hitting the ball did not seem so very difficult. She might possibly distinguish herself even amongst these Philistines.

Lydia, in fact, was not above coveting the admiration of those whom she admittedly despised.

"Chuck you an easy one to start with," shouted Olive, good-naturedly.

Lydia jerked up the bat, but heard no reassuring contact with the slow moving ball.

"Don't spoon it up like that! You'd have been caught out for a dead cert if you had hit it!"

A second attempt was made.

"You *are* a duffer! Show her how to hold the bat, someone."

Lydia's third effort mysteriously succeeded in knocking down the improvised stumps behind her, whilst the ball, still unhit, was neatly caught by a nine-year-old Swaine child.

"Oh, I say, this is awfully slow!" remonstrated Bob.

"She's out now, anyway."

"Give her another chance," said Olive, "let her finish the over, anyway. There's no scoring, what's it matter?"

"Two more balls, then."

But there was only one more ball. Lydia, desperately determined to succeed once at least, exerted her whole strength miraculously, hit the ball fair and square, and knew a momentary triumph as it flew off the bat.

There was an ear-piercing shriek from Olive, and Lydia, terrified, saw her fling up both hands to her face and stagger round and round where she stood.

"Oh, I say, are you hurt, ole gurl?" came in anxious, if rather obvious, inquiry from the surrounding field.

"Got her bang on the jaw!"

"What awful rot, poor wretch."

They crowded round Olive, who was choking and gulping, her mouth streaming with blood, but undauntedly gasping:

"It's all right, don't fuss, I tell you, Bee, it's all right. I'll be all right in a sec. I never dreamt she was going to hit out like that. I ought to have caught it."

"Comes of having a mouth like a pound of liver splits," said Bob, quite unconsciously making use of the strain of facetious personal incivility always used by him to any intimate, and all the while solicitously patting his sister on the back.

"Oh, *Olive*, I'm so sorry," said Lydia, far more acutely aware than anyone else was likely to be of the inadequacy of the time-worn formula.

"Don't be an ass," returned Olive crisply. "Lend me a nose wipe if you want to do something useful. Mine's soaked."

Such of the assembly as were possessed of pocket-handkerchiefs willingly sacrificed them, although the number contributed proved utterly inadequate to the amount of blood lost by Olive, still determinedly making light of her injuries.

"Let's have a look and see if your teeth are all out, old gurl," urged Beatrice.

"I lost two last summer," the eldest Swaine remarked casually, "and Dot had one knocked out at hockey."

"The front one feels a bit loose," said Olive thoughtfully, and thrust a finger and thumb into a rapidly swelling mouth.

"Better not push it about," someone suggested; "why not sit down and have tea now?"

"You don't want to go home, do you, Ol?" Lydia heard Beatrice ask her sister aside.

"Good Lord, no. Don't let's have any *fuss*."

Olive could certainly not be accused of making the most of her distressing circumstances.

She gave Lydia a tremendous bang on the back, and said:

"Cheer up, old stupid! You jolly well don't pretend you can't hit out when you want to another time, that's all!"

After that she took her place amongst the others, and contrived to eat a great deal of bread-and-butter and several of the softer variety of cakes, in spite of the evident possibilities of a swelled and discoloured upper lip and badly bruised jaw.

"Old Olive has plenty of pluck—I will say that for her," Bob remarked to Lydia, who agreed with the more fervour that she was conscious of a quite involuntary sort of jealousy of Olive. It must be so much pleasanter to be the injured than the injurer, and to know that everyone was, at least inwardly, approving one's courage and powers of endurance.

When the picnic was over, Olive had quite a large escort to accompany her home, all relating in loud and cheerful voices the various disabilities and disfigurements that had sooner or later overtaken them in the pursuit of athletic enjoyment.

"It's part of the fun," declared Olive herself. "I only hope the mater won't turn green at the sight of me. She's a bit squeamish sometimes."

"Hold your hand in front of your mouth."

"Keep your back to the light all you can."

But it became evident that none of these precautions would avail when Mrs. Senthoven was seen leaning over the gate, gazing down the road.

She waved a yellow envelope at them.

"Tellywag!" exclaimed Beatrice. "What on earth can it be?"

Telegrams were so rare in the Wimbledon establishment as to be looked upon with alarm.

She and Olive both began to run.

"It's addressed to you, Lydia," screamed Beatrice. "Come and open it. Come on, you people."

The last exhortation was in encouragement to the members of the Swaine family, delicately hanging back. At Beatrice's semaphore-like gesticulations of invitation, they all followed Lydia's rush forward, and as she opened her telegram she heard their loud babble uprise.

"Not so bad as it looks, is it, Ol?"

"She got a swipe on the jaw, and took it like a brick, too!"

"Oh, my dear girl!" from Aunt Evelyn. "Let me look this minute——"

"Don't fuss, mater. It's all right, really."

They were all pressing round the reluctant Olive.

Lydia looked up.

"No bad news, I hope, dear," said Aunt Evelyn, as was her invariable custom whenever present at the opening of a telegram.

"It's from Aunt Beryl about my examination," said Lydia very clearly.

She was so much excited that her tense, distinct utterance produced a sudden silence, and they all looked at her.

"*Passed your examination first-class honours*," read Lydia out loud.

"I *say*!"

"And you'd been ill the whole time, hadn't you? My golly!"

"Why, we thought you hadn't a chance!"

"Weren't you the youngest one there, or some rot of that kind?"

"First-class honours! That's as high as you can go, isn't it?"

They were all lavish of exclamations and hearty slangy congratulations.

Olive herself, and everybody else, had forgotten all about Olive's injury, and Lydia was the centre of attention.

"I say, let's have a celebration!" shouted Bob. "Come in after supper and have a cocoa-rag."

The invitation was accepted with loud enthusiasm.

"You can have the dining-room, dears," said Aunt Evelyn, "only not too much noise, because of father. I'll explain it to him, and get him to sit in the drawing-room."

Uncle Robert never took part in any festivity of his family's. It was supposed that he needed peace and solitude after his day's work, and in summer he pottered about the little green-house, and at other times of the year dozed behind the newspaper, unmolested. Nevertheless, Uncle Robert, to Lydia's astonishment and gratification, actually came out of his taciturnity that evening at supper-time in order to pay tribute to her achievement.

"Fancy the pater waking up like that!" ejaculated Bob afterwards. "More than he's ever done for any of us."

"A fat lot of exams. we've ever passed!" said Beatrice scornfully.

It was true that no Senthoven had ever attained to any such distinction, and Lydia realized with the more surprise that for this very reason they regarded her success as something nearly approaching to the miraculous.

Almost against her own will, she was struck with Olive's unfeigned relief at having the general attention distracted from herself and her accident, and focussed instead upon her cousin's triumph.

Lydia half admired and half despised Olive, and most wholly and thoroughly enjoyed the novel sensation of being for once of high account in the eyes of the Wimbledon household.

Certainly towards the end of the exceedingly rowdy "celebration," the cause of it was rather lost sight of in the fumes of unlimited cocoa, the shrieking giggles of the younger Swaine children, and the uproarious mirth of their seniors, the whole-hearted amusement, that almost seemed as though it would never be stayed, at so exquisitely humorous an accident as the collapse of Bob's chair beneath him.

Nevertheless, the celebration was all in Lydia's honour, and her health was drunk in very hot, very thick cocoa, with a great deal of coarse brown sediment at the bottom of each cup, afterwards scraped up into a spoon, and forcibly administered to the youngest child present, who had rashly declared a liking for "grounds."

Lydia, highly excited, for once made as much noise as anybody, and began to feel that she should be quite sorry to say good-bye to them all on Monday.

But she was much too clear-sighted in the analysis of her own situations to delude herself into supposing that a prolongation of her stay at Wimbledon would result in anything but failure.

One could not pass an examination with brilliancy every day, and once the first sensation over—which it speedily would be—the old routine of walks and hockey and "ragging" would go on as before, and Lydia could no longer hope for anything but, at best, a negative obscurity. Far better to leave them before any of their gratifying enthusiasm had had time to die down.

She could tell, by the very nature of their farewells, the immense difference that now obtained in their estimation of her importance.

"You must go on as well as you've begun, Lydia. It's a great thing for a girl to be clever," said Aunt Evelyn rather wistfully. "I suppose you'll want to take up teaching, later on?"

"Perhaps. I'm not quite sure yet."

Lydia had long ago given up talking about her childish ambition to write books, although it was stronger than ever within her.

"Well, there's time to settle yet. You're not sixteen, and there's no hurry. I'm sure Grandpapa and Aunt Beryl would miss you dreadfully if you thought of going away anywhere. It would be best if you could get something to do down there, wouldn't it?"

"Yes, Aunt Evelyn," said Lydia amiably. She always listened to older people politely and agreed with what they said, but their advice had no disturbing effect upon her, because it never seriously occurred to her that anyone could be a better judge of her own interests than she was herself.

Even Uncle Robert, hastily saying good-bye before starting for the office, found time to say to her:

"Well, good-bye, child. Don't overwork yourself with all this examination stuff. You can come down here if you want a change any time. Settle it with your aunt."

"Better come down for the Christmas hols. We can show you some tobogganing then, most likely. I got some whopping great bruises on my legs last year," was the inducement held out by Olive. "I must be off to that beastly old holiday task now, I suppose. I always put it off to the last minute. Wish I was a stew-pot like you."

Beatrice and Bob escorted Lydia to the station.

"Well, ta-ta, and be a good girl," said Bob patronizingly, tilting his hat rather far back on his head and smoking a cigarette that aggressively protruded from the extreme corner of his mouth, "when's the old man going to have the decency to remember my existence? You've cut us all out with him with your blooming book-work. He goes in for being a bit of a brainy old bird himself, doesn't he?"

Inured though she might be to the Senthoven vocabulary, Lydia nearly shuddered visibly at the thought of Grandpapa, had he heard his descendant's description of him.

"Shut up, you ass," said Beatrice, in an automatic sort of way. "Well, bye-bye, ole gurl. You've fixed it up with the mater about popping down again some time, I s'pose. Just come and take us as you find us, as the saying goes. Here's your train."

Lydia, leaning from the window of the third-class railway carriage, wondered whether to shake hands with Beatrice or not. The law of "No nonsense about *us*" would certainly preclude kissing, even had she felt the slightest desire to embrace her rough-haired, freckle-faced cousin, shifting from one leg to the other, her red hands thrust into the pockets of her woollen coat, and her tam o' shanter pulled well down over one eye.

Bob was already casting glances in the direction of the refreshment room.

"Good-bye," said Lydia, definitely deciding against putting out her hand. "And thanks so much."

"Good heavens! Don't start speechifying, whatever you do," cried the Senthovens in protesting horror, both at the same moment, and as nearly as possible in the same words.

So Lydia was obliged to have recourse to that most uncomfortable form of ejaculatory conversation that appears to be incumbent upon all those who are unfortunate enough to be accompanied by their friends to the railway station.

"Nearly off now, I think."

"Oh, yes, there's the whistle."

"Well, I suppose Aunt Beryl will expect us to send our love, or some rot of that kind."

"All right. I think we really *are* starting this time."

We were not, however, and Lydia looked dumbly at her waiting cousins and wondered why, since they had nothing more to say, and were obviously quite as ill at ease as she was herself, they did not go.

"I wish you wouldn't wait. We shall be off in a minute now."

"Oh, it's all right."

Beatrice shifted her weight on to the other leg, and Bob pulled out a packet of Woodbine cigarettes and lit one of them.

"I hope Grandpapa will be in good form," said Bob desperately.

"I'll tell him you asked."

"Oh, don't bother."

"He knows there isn't any nonsense about *us*," said Beatrice.

To this last familiar refrain, the train actually began to move out of the station at last. Lydia waved her hand once or twice, received curt nods in reply, and sank back with a feeling of relief on to her seat.

The end of the Senthovens.

She could not help feeling glad that her visit was over.

The familiar quiet of Regency Terrace awaited her now. Aunt Beryl, as her letters had assured Lydia, once more returned to the unobtrusive rôle out of which her illness had momentarily forced her into unsuitable lime-light. Uncle George, certain to be full of quiet pride in the result of the examination, even Mr. Monteagle Almond, next Wednesday, probably framing elaborate little congratulatory sentences.

Lydia looked forward intensely to it all.

She wondered how Grandpapa would receive her, and mentally conned over the amusing descriptions that she would give him in private of the Senthoven *ménage*, treading upon his well-known prejudice against that slang in the use of which it was so proficient.

She did not expect to be met at the station, but sent her luggage by the omnibus, and herself walked to Regency Terrace by the short cut, remembering as she did so her arrival, more than three years ago, under the care of both aunts, and full of uncertainty as to her own eventual destination.

Security, reflected Lydia maturely, was the most important thing of all. One was secure where one was appreciated, and held to be of importance.

She remembered that it was upon her own representations that Grandpapa had consented—going against his own prejudice to do so—to her being sent to school. It had been a great success, as even Grandpapa must have long ago acknowledged to himself.

Perhaps one day he might even acknowledge it to her.

Lydia smiled to herself over the improbability of the suggestion.

Then she turned the corner into Regency Terrace and saw the familiar house on the opposite side of the road.

As she caught sight of it, the hall-door opened, and Aunt Beryl, in her well-known blue foulard dress with white spots, that she generally only wore on Sundays, looked out. At the same instant Lydia saw Grandpapa peering from the dining-room window, which was already open, and raising his stick a few inches in the air to shake it in welcome.

All in honour of the great examination victory!

Lydia waved her hand excitedly, and at the same moment, with ear-piercing barks, Shamrock shot out from behind Aunt Beryl, trailing a significant length of broken chain behind him, and raced madly down the road towards her.

Lydia, breaking into quick, irrepressible laughter, dashed across the road and up the steps, in sudden, acute happiness at so vivid a realization of her dreams of home-coming.

VI

TIME slipped by with mysterious rapidity.

Lydia was in the sixth form—she was a prefect—she was Head of the School.

At seventeen she discovered that she had ceased to grow. She had attained to her full height, and after all, it was not the outrageous stature that had been prophesied for her. Only five feet eight inches, and her slimness, and the smallness of her bones, made her look less tall.

Her thick, brown hair was in one plait now, doubled under and tied with a black ribbon, and her skirts reached down to her slender ankles.

Lydia still had doubts as to her own claims to beauty, and envied Nathalie Palmer her bright, Devonshire complexion and blue eyes.

"Should you say I was *at all* pretty, Nathalie?"

"Your eyes are lovely."

"That's what people always say about plain girls," said Lydia disgustedly.

"You look sort of foreign, and interesting," said Nathalie thoughtfully. "The shape of your face is quite different to anyone else's."

It did not sound reassuring, and Lydia touched with the tips of her fingers the salient cheek bones that gave an odd hint of Mongolianism to her small olive-hued face.

"Your mouth is pretty, it's so red," said Nathalie. "Though I should like it better if your teeth didn't slope inwards."

Nathalie adored Lydia, but she was incurably honest.

She went home for good the year before Lydia was to enter upon her last term at Miss Glover's.

"You'll come and stay with us next year, won't you?" entreated Nathalie. "There's no one but father and me at home, but quite a lot of nice people live near."

"Of course I'll come. I'd love to come. I should just have left here," said Lydia.

She wondered whether Nathalie realized that on leaving school she would be seeking for employment. Most of Miss Glover's pupils had their homes in the locality, and went as a matter of course "to help father in the shop." Several found situations as teachers, one had gone to Bristol University to study for a medical degree, and only a minority, like Nathalie herself, looked forward to living at home.

Lydia knew that she meant to write, and she had long ago told Nathalie the secret of her ambitions, but she had said nothing about other work, and the two girls parted without having broached the subject.

"It will be time enough to tell Nathalie when I know what I'm going to do," reflected Lydia, with characteristic caution.

She was sure that Aunt Beryl expected her to teach. Miss Glover herself had hinted that a post as Junior Mistress might be available in a year's time to one of Lydia's abilities. That would mean sleeping at home, having long holidays in the summer, and lesser ones at Christmas and Easter, and a salary as well as her midday dinner at school.

It might also mean a Senior Mistress-ship after a certain number of years, an increase of salary, and the far-away, ultimate possibility of partnership with the Head. And it would also mean an endless succession of pupils, almost all local, a life spent among femininity until her interests would all centre round numbers of her own sex, and a narrowing of vision such as must be inevitable in a mind exclusively engaged in intercourse with the half-developed faculties of youth.

Lydia wished to leave the little seaside town.

Regency Terrace should be her home; she wanted to come back there for holidays, and to receive the proud welcome that had awaited her after her visit to Wimbledon, when she had passed her examination with first-class honours.

But her secret determination was to find work in London. Only in London, thought Lydia, would her vaunted capabilities be put to the test. Only there could she hope to come into contact with that strata of life, somehow different to the one in which Aunt Beryl, or the Jacksons, or the Senthovens moved, and to which, she felt inwardly certain, she herself would be acclaimed instantly as by right divine. Finally, only in the immensities of London did Lydia think that she would gain the experience necessary for the fulfilment of her desire to write.

Hitherto her keen critical faculty had left her exceedingly dissatisfied with her own literary attempts.

Once at sixteen years old, she had entered a competition started by a girl's paper for a short story "dealing with animal life." Lydia had first of all written a long and exciting account of a runaway elephant in the jungle in India, with a little English boy—chota-sahib—on its back.

Aunt Beryl's praises, which had been enthusiastic, had failed to satisfy her, owing, Lydia supposed, to her own intimate conviction of Aunt Beryl's lack of discrimination.

But she had disconcertingly found that it would be utterly impossible to submit the story to Grandpapa's discerning ear and incisive judgment.

Why?

Lydia, disregarding a certain violent inclination to shelve the whole question, had ruthlessly analyzed her feelings of discomfort at the very idea of hearing Grandpapa's comments upon her work. There was no doubt of it—Grandpapa would say that Lydia knew nothing about India, or runaway elephants, or chota-sahibs—she had suddenly writhed, remembering the very book of travels in which she first met with that expression—that her story was all written at second or third hand, and was therefore worthless. With a courage that afterwards struck her as surprising, Lydia had envisaged the horrid truth.

She had lacked the heart to destroy the runaway elephant altogether, but had stuffed the manuscript out of sight into the back of her writing-table drawer, and resolutely sat down to consider whether she could not lay claim to any first-hand impressions of animal life.

The result had been a short, humorously written sketch of one of Shamrock's innumerable escapades.

Lydia had not been awarded the first prize, as she inwardly felt would have been in accordance with the dramatic fitness of things, but she had thoroughly amused Grandpapa by reading the sketch to him aloud, and she had taught herself a valuable lesson.

Experience, she had decided sweepingly, was the only royal road to literature. She would write no more until experience was hers.

Experience, however, to Lydia's way of thinking, was not to be gained by remaining at Regency Terrace for ever.

When the last of her school days was approaching rapidly, she decided that the time had come to speak.

"Grandpapa, I should like to ask your advice."

"Light the gas, my dear. Your aunt is very late out this afternoon," was Grandpapa's only reply.

When Grandpapa simulated deafness, it always meant that he

was displeased.

Lydia obediently struck a match, and the gas, through its crinkly pink globe, threw a sudden spurt of light all over the familiar dining-room.

Grandpapa leant stiffly back in his arm-chair, a tiny, waxen-looking figure, with alert eyes that seemed oddly youthful and mischievous, seen above his knotted hands and shrunken limbs. He could see and hear whatever he pleased, but it was becoming more and more difficult for him to move, although he still staunchly refused to be helped from his chair.

"Lyddie, where's Shamrock?"

Useless to reply, as was in fact the case, "I don't know." The futility of such a reply was bound to call forth one of Grandpapa's most disconcerting sarcasms.

"I'll find out, Grandpapa."

Luck favoured Lydia.

As a rule, one might as well attempt to follow the course of a comet as that of Shamrock's illicit excursions. But on this occasion Lydia at once found him in the hall, and was so much relieved at the prospect of success with Shamrock's owner, that she failed to take notice of the stealthy manner of Shamrock's approach, denoting a distinct consciousness of wrong-doing.

"Good little dog!" said Grandpapa delightedly. "They talk a great deal of nonsense about his sneaking off into the town and stealing from the shops—I don't believe a word of it! He's always here when *I* want him."

At which Shamrock fawned enthusiastically upon his master, and Lydia determined the hour to be a propitious one, and began again:

"Will you give me your advice, Grandpapa?"

"Lyddie, you said that a little while ago," said Grandpapa severely. "It's a foolish feminine way of speaking, and I thought you had more sense."

Lydia looked at her disconcerting grandparent in silence.

She knew herself far better able to steer clear of his many and violent prejudices than was matter-of-fact Uncle George, or unfortunate Aunt Beryl, who often seemed to go out of her way in order to fall foul of them. But this time she was conscious of perplexity.

"I don't understand, Grandpapa. I really *do* want your advice."

"Advice is cheap," said Grandpapa. "A great many people say they want it, especially women. What they really want, Lyddie, is an opportunity for telling someone what they have already decided to do. Then they can say afterwards 'Oh, but so-and-so and I talked it *all* over and he advised me to do such-and-such.' You mark my word, no one ever yet asked advice whose mind wasn't more or less made up already."

To take the bull by the horns was always the best way of dealing with Grandpapa.

Lydia said resolutely:

"Well, I haven't yet made up my mind, Grandpapa, that's why I want to talk to you."

"So that I can advise you to do whatever you want to do?" satirically demanded Grandpapa. "Well, my dear, you know me well enough to know that I shan't do *that*. Talk away."

Thus encouraged, Lydia began.

"I am seventeen, Grandpapa."

She pretended not to hear Grandpapa's cheerful ejaculation, "Only seventeen, my dear? Quite a young child, then."

"I shall be eighteen by the time I leave school next month, and there'll be my future to think about. I know Miss Glover means to give me a chance of a Junior Mistress-ship, or I suppose I could get a post as governess, as Aunt Beryl is always suggesting. It would be a pity to waste all my education at dressmaking, or anything like that, though I suppose I *could* take up something of the sort. Only really I feel as though I'd rather use my head than my hands. Of course, I like anything to do with figures, and Mr. Almond seemed to think that I shouldn't have any difficulty in getting into the Bank here."

She paused.

"Well," said Grandpapa, "you've told me all the things you *don't* mean to do. Now tell me what you've really decided."

Lydia, although rather angry, could not help laughing outright, and immediately felt that her laughter had done herself and her cause more good than any amount of eloquence. Eloquence indeed was invariably wasted upon Grandpapa, who preferred any good speaking that might take place to be done by himself.

"Now, child, have done with this nonsense and speak out. What is it you want?"

Lydia drew a long breath.

"To go and work in London."

There was a long pause, and then Grandpapa said in rather a flat voice:

"So that's it, is it? Well, well, well—who'd have thought it?"

"Grandpapa! you didn't think I should stay here *always*?" protested Lydia. "How am I ever to get any experience, in one place all the time, never seeing any new people?"

"'Never' is a long day," quoth Grandpapa.

"But I shall have to begin soon if I'm to work at all. You and Aunt Beryl have always said that I must do something when I leave school."

"And supposing I said now that things have looked up a little, and you could live at home and help your aunt a bit, and take little Shamrock out of a morning. Eh, Lyddie, what then?"

Lydia was silent, but she did not attempt to conceal that her face fell at the suggestion.

"Well, well, well," said Grandpapa again, "so it's to be London!"

"Then you'll let me go," Lydia exclaimed, trying to keep the eagerness out of her voice.

Grandpapa uttered one of his most disagreeable, croaking laughs.

"Don't talk like a little fool, my dear! You know very well that if you want to go, you'll go. How can I prevent it? I am only an old man."

Lydia was disconcerted. Grandpapa never spoke of himself as old, and the hint of pathos in the admission, unintentional though she supposed it to be, seemed to her out of place in the present juncture.

She grew more annoyed as the evening wore on, for Grandpapa was really very tiresome.

"A useless old man, that's what I am," he soliloquized, taking care, however, to make himself perfectly audible.

"What is the matter, Grandpapa?" said the much surprised Aunt Beryl.

Everyone knew how angry Grandpapa would have been had he suspected anyone else of looking upon him as a useless old man.

"Anno Domini," sighed Grandpapa melodramatically, "Anno Domini! No one left but little Shamrock to keep the old man company."

"Grandpapa!" cried Aunt Beryl indignantly, "I'm sure if you had to depend on the dog for company, you *might* complain. But you know very well that isn't the case. Why, here's George only too ready to have a game of Halma, if you want to. Or Lydia could read out to you for a bit."

"Lyddie's off to London, my dear," sighed Grandpapa in martyred accents, for all the world, thought Lydia indignantly, as though she meant to start off by the next train.

"*What?*"

But Grandpapa, having dropped his bomb amongst them, not unwisely elected to leave it there without waiting to see its effect.

"I shall go up to bed now, my boy. Will you give me an arm?"

"But it's quite early. Don't you feel well, Grandpapa? And what's all this about Lydia going away?"

Aunt Beryl received no answer.

Lydia was too much vexed and too much embarrassed to make any attempt at stating her case, and Grandpapa had begun the tense process of hoisting himself out of his arm-chair. When he was on his feet at last, he allowed Uncle George to come and assist him out of the room and up the stairs.

"Good night all," said Grandpapa in a sorrowful, impersonal sort of way, as he hobbled out of the room on his son's arm. "I am getting to be an old fellow now—I can't afford to keep late hours. Bed and gruel, that's all that's left for the old man."

Aunt Beryl looked at Lydia with dismay.

"What's all this about? Grandpapa hasn't been like this since he was so vexed that time when Uncle George took Shamrock out and lost him, and he was away three days before a policeman brought him back. I remember Grandpapa going on in just the same way then, talking about being an old man and nobody caring for him. Such nonsense!"

Lydia had seldom heard so much indignation expressed by her quiet aunt, and for a moment she hoped that attention might be diverted from her own share in the disturbance of Grandpapa's serenity.

But an early recollection of the unfortunate effects upon Aunt Beryl of her withheld confidence, five years previously, came to her mind. Lydia considered the position quietly for a few moments, and then decided upon her line of attack.

"I know you'll understand much better than Grandpapa did, and help me with him," she began.

Not for nothing had the child Lydia learnt the necessity for diplomacy in dealing with those arbitrary controllers of Destiny called grown-up people.

Aunt Beryl seemed a good deal startled, and perhaps rather disappointed, which Lydia indulgently told herself was natural enough, but the subtle appeal to range herself with her niece against Grandpapa's overdone pretensions was not without its effect.

And Lydia found an unexpected ally in Uncle George, when her scheme had presently reached the stage of family discussion.

"You ought to get a good post enough," he said judicially, "but you mustn't expect to keep yourself all at once unless you 'live in' somewhere!"

"If she goes to London at all," Aunt Beryl said firmly, "she must go to Maria Nettleship."

Of course. Maria Nettleship, the *amie d'enfance* of Aunt Beryl's younger days, who still punctually exchanged letters with her, and was successfully managing a boarding-house in Bloomsbury.

"I should be happier about her with Maria Nettleship than if she was just 'living in' with goodness knows whom to keep her company. And it's *nicer*, too, for a young girl like Lydia—you know what I mean," said Aunt Beryl mysteriously.

"But a boarding-house is expensive. I never thought of anything like that, auntie. Why, I should cost you more than I would if I lived at home, a great deal," said Lydia, aghast.

"Oh, I could easily make an arrangement with Maria Nettleship. And you want the chance, Lydia, my dear. I'm sure I don't blame you. It's not a good thing to stay in one place all one's life long, I suppose." Aunt Beryl gave a sigh. "It would be just an experiment for a little while, and I'm sure the expense isn't to be thought of when we know you would be paying it all back in a year or two."

"If it's simply a question of the ready," said Uncle George solemnly, "I can lay my hand on something at the minute. A bachelor has few expenses, and except for the little I make over to the house, I can put by a tidy little bit every year. I should look upon it as quite a profitable investment, Lydia, I assure you, to provide the needful on this occasion."

"Oh, Uncle George—thank you very much. But haven't I any money at all of my own without having to take yours?" cried Lydia, distressed.

Uncle George shook his head.

"Your poor mother was very unwise in the management of her affairs—very unwise indeed. There's a matter of twenty or twenty-five pounds coming to you every year, Lydia, and that's about all."

"Did that pay for my being sent to school?"

"There was a little money of your father's, that he left to me," said Aunt Beryl hastily. "I was always his favourite sister, whatever Evelyn may say, and it seemed only natural that his child should have the benefit of it, I'm sure. Now leave that, my dear, and tell me what sort of work you think of looking out for in town."

"Certainly," said Uncle George, "that must be all cut and dried before you think of starting off."

Lydia felt almost bewildered by the rapidity with which things appeared to be settling themselves. A boarding-house in London, independent work, and leisure and opportunity for the writing that was to bring her fame and money! She remembered once more, and this time with triumph, Grandpapa's old assertion: "There's no such thing as *can't*."

Lydia's determination to succeed, product partly of an ambitious and resolute character, and partly of sheer ignorance as to the difficulties that might lie in wait for her, was enhanced by an ardent desire to justify the astonishingly practical belief in her that Aunt Beryl and Uncle George were displaying.

Uncle George, who was not at all in the habit of paying compliments, even said to her:

"I must say, it isn't every girl who would have the courage to start life as you're proposing to do, Lydia, and you deserve every success, I'm sure."

After this, it was a disagreeable shock to find that another, and entirely opposite, point of view could be taken of her venture.

One Wednesday evening, to Lydia's infinite surprise, silent, dried-up little Mr. Monteagle Almond suddenly broached the subject. He chose his opportunity with evident care. Grandpapa, who still elected to maintain his pose of rapidly-approaching dissolution, had waited until the first game of chess was in full swing, and then demanded plaintively if his son was too busy amusing himself to give the poor old man an arm upstairs.

"Excuse me one moment, Monty."

Uncle George had departed dutifully.

Almost at the same moment the maid Gertrude had put her head round the door, the rest of her remaining outside the room, after the fashion most deplored by Miss Raymond, and given breathless utterance:

"Oh, miss! Could you come out a minute, please? Shamrock's got his head squeezed in between the railings at the back, and I can't get him out, and he's howling something awful!"

"That dog!"

Permitting herself only this forbearing exclamation, Aunt Beryl also had hastened away.

Mr. Monteagle Almond remained seated before the chess-table, sedulously tracing a little imaginary pattern on the board with one long yellow forefinger.

Lydia was seated under the gas, which she had turned up as high as it would go, absorbed in finishing a Sunday blouse for herself.

"I am sorry to hear of your projected departure, Miss Lydia," suddenly said Mr. Monteagle Almond. "Quite a break-up of the home circle."

"Oh, no!" protested Lydia, who would have been more deeply concerned at this fashion of viewing her going if she had not been accustomed to Mr. Almond's sententious phraseology on every occasion. "Besides, I'm not going yet. It's only a plan for next winter perhaps. I shan't leave school until the end of this term."

Mr. Almond shook his head.

"A great wrench for old Mr. Raymond no doubt, and he seems to me to be breaking up. To-night, for instance, he was quite tremulous. I was sorry to see that."

"So was I," muttered Lydia rather viciously. It was really too bad of Grandpapa to put on those airs that would take in anyone who did not know all of which he was capable.

"The old are perhaps less apt at concealing their feelings than we younger folk," pursued Mr. Almond. "Now, I'm sure my good friends, your aunt and uncle, have not allowed you to see how deeply your decision will affect them."

"They've been very kind," said Lydia with emphasis. She was anxious that no one should think her ungrateful.

"I have no doubt of it at all—none whatever. A most kind-hearted fellow is George—most kind-hearted. And as for Miss Raymond—well, I need not tell you what she is. I am sure that you remember her devoted nursing of you—for which she afterwards suffered so severely—on the occasion of some childish ailment of yours a couple of years ago."

Mr. Almond fixed an eye of melancholy severity upon Lydia, looking as though he were much less sure than he alleged himself to be of her remembering the occasion in question, and was consequently determined to recall it to her memory.

Lydia was speechless with indignation.

Pneumonia a childish ailment!

One of the chief crises of her youth to be recalled merely as the setting for the jewel of Aunt Beryl's self-devotion!

Mr. Almond was worse than Grandpapa even.

It was clear to her that here was a point of view which required readjustment.

"I shall be very, very sorry to leave home," she said earnestly. "But indeed I do think it's the best thing I can do. If I get a good post in London, it will lead to much more than my just going on at Miss Glover's, teaching, for ever. And it seems a shame not to make the very most of the education I've had."

"Very true. But I'm afraid you'll be sadly missed. One had

hoped, if I may say so without offence, to see you taking your aunt's place in time. She has been very much tied now for a number of years."

"I *do* hope to help Aunt Beryl. But it would be a disappointment to her and to Uncle George if I didn't do something with the education they've given me. In some ways," said Lydia, "the thought of going to London by myself frightens me—but honestly, Mr. Almond, I believe if I once take the plunge, it'll turn out to be the best and most profitable for us all in the long run."

She saw by his face, with decided relief, that the little man was becoming mollified.

"I'm glad you look at it in that light. You'll excuse me speaking like this, I hope, but I'll admit to you, Miss Lydia, that at first I was inclined to think you might be going into this without much thought for anyone but yourself. What you've just said shows me that I may have misjudged you."

"Indeed," Lydia said deferentially, "I know it's only from friendship that you're saying it at all. But I hope you'll believe that I really am not ungrateful to them all—and I do want to make them proud of me. I hope I shall, too, if I have my chance."

The middle-aged bank clerk looked at her with a gaze that seemed half admiring and half envious.

"Well," he said slowly, "they're giving you your chance all right, Miss Lydia. And I hope, if I may say so, that you'll make the most of it, both for your own sake and for theirs."

And Lydia, whilst agreeing with him in all sincerity, felt with an odd sense of triumph that she had reinstated herself in the good opinion of the loyal friend of the family.

This opinion received a startling confirmation the next time that she saw him.

"Have you decided upon the exact nature of your employment in London?" he inquired of her, with an air of caution.

"Oh, no. I don't very much care for the idea of teaching, and I should have to learn shorthand and typewriting before I could get secretarial work. What I should really like would be something to do with figures—accountancy perhaps."

"Ah! I thought so. The mathematical mind! A very rare thing in your sex," said Mr. Monteagle Almond, as he had frequently said before. "But subject to the approval of your good aunt, I have here something that may interest you, I think."

Aunt Beryl and Lydia gazed eagerly at the paper he held out to them, covered with telegraphic notes written in Mr. Almond's neat little clerkly hand.

"New venture. *Robes et Modes.* Started last year. Establishment owned by Lady Proprietress, personally known to informant. Prem. in West End already acquired and cap. assured."

"Opening for educ. young lady; a/cs and help in sales-room when required."

"Live out; midday meal in. Special feature made of employees' welfare."

"Personal interview previous to engagt. Probably Sept. Salary to begin—no premium."

"Only superior young ladies considered."

"The last item," said Mr. Almond solemnly, "was much dwelt upon by my informant—Griswell, of the N. S. Bank. He could give me very few details, but seeing that I was interested, he immediately offered to communicate with the lady concerned, a personal friend of his. He merely mentioned her name to me by chance, and was quite surprised at my taking him up, like."

"It was very kind of you to pass it on, I'm sure," said Aunt Beryl excitedly. "What do you say about it, Lydia?"

"I should like, if Mr. Almond will be so very kind, to hear all about it," said Lydia, her eyes shining and her heart full of excitement.

VII

"WELL, Lyddie, I hope you'll find enjoyment in trimming bonnets for fine ladies," said Grandpapa caustically.

"She's to keep the accounts, Grandpapa," Aunt Beryl repeated in loud, displeased accents. "Nothing to do with the millinery, naturally."

"I'm not so sure of that—not so sure of that. What did the old party say about helping in the shop?"

"Madame Ribeiro only asked if Lydia would be willing to give a hand at sale-time, or anything like that, and of course she agreed. It's her book-keeping they want."

"And who is Madame Ribeiro?"

"Oh, Grandpapa!" cried Lydia reproachfully, "you know very well that Aunt Beryl and I went up to town this morning on purpose to see her. She's the old lady who owns the shop, and wants to run it on new lines. Why, she's a sort of lady, isn't she, Aunt Beryl?"

"It's a foreign name," was the indirect, but distrustful, reply of Aunt Beryl. "I didn't like to ask her what country she belonged to, quite. Is it a French name?"

"Portuguese," said Grandpapa unexpectedly. "There are Ribeiros all over the Dutch East Indies."

"She seemed a nice person enough—older than I expected, and dressed very quietly in black, like a widow. She certainly had a moustache, but then some of those very dark foreigners *are* like that, and I'm sure it's her misfortune, and not her fault, poor thing—like her stoutness."

"She talked very, very slowly, and with an accent," Lydia said. "She never smiled once, either—I never saw such a solemn face, and enormous black eyes. But I think I should like her."

"But it's she that's got to like you," Grandpapa pointed out. "You've got to work at the bonnets under her, haven't you, Lyddie?"

"Not exactly under her. She doesn't come to the shop herself, much—someone she calls Madame Elena is in charge there. Madame Ribeiro lives in her own house, in St. John's Wood. But the shop is hers, and she engages all the helpers herself. She sees them all personally."

"And is this precious shop in St. John's Wood, too?"

"Certainly not. It's in the West End," said Aunt Beryl with dignity.

"Then I suppose Lyddie would like a little house in Park Lane, so as to be near it?" Grandpapa inquired with an air of simplicity.

"I thought I told you that Lydia was going to Maria Nettleship's," said Aunt Beryl stiffly.

"I wish we'd had time to go and see Miss Nettleship," cried Lydia, hastily turning the conversation.

She did not in the least mind Grandpapa's sarcasms herself—in fact, she was rather amused by them—but they always greatly discomposed Aunt Beryl.

But when a definite offer had been made by letter and accepted, and it was decided that Lydia was to go, much sooner than they had expected, to London, and work at the accountancy in the shop that old Madame Ribeiro called "Elena's," she determined to have some sort of an explanation with Grandpapa.

It worried her very much to see that he regarded this first step in her career as a mere wilful, childish freak, and something of a personal injury to himself.

The spirit of Uncle George and Aunt Beryl was a very different one. They praised her courage and determination in starting out into the world by herself, and were full of pride in the letters so willingly supplied by Miss Glover and Dr. Young, and the clergyman who had prepared Lydia for confirmation, all setting forth her cleverness, and her steady ways and the achievements that lay to her credit in scholarship. They were proud of her for having obtained so quickly a post at a salary of a pound a week to begin with, and her midday dinner and tea five times a week—which practically brought it up to twenty-five shillings a week, Uncle George pointed out. They would only allow her to pay half of the weekly salary to Miss Nettleship. The rest—an additional ten shillings—Uncle George insisted that he should remit to Lydia by postal order every Friday.

"That will leave you something for 'bus fares, and dress expenses," he said. "And I shouldn't like you to touch your own income, child. Let that accumulate for a rainy day."

"You can't hope to save much at first, you know," said Aunt Beryl. "But you're well off for clothes, and won't want anything new except the black dress they said you'd need, and I can make over the old *broche* easily enough. It's beautiful stuff—you'll only have to get the cambric for the neck and sleeves. It's a great help to a girl when she can do her own dressmaking."

They could think of nothing but Lydia.

Mr. Monteagle Almond himself, who had procured this fine chance for her, was hardly given any credit by Lydia's uncle and aunt. They ascribed it all to her own merits.

Lydia quite longed to justify all this faith in her, and to repay Uncle George and Aunt Beryl for their sacrifice. But she did not really feel much doubt of being able to do so eventually.

This made Grandpapa's attitude the more vexatious.

"I shall be able to come home for Christmas, you know, Grandpapa," she said one day.

"Where are we now—August? And they want you to begin at the end of this month?"

"That's so that I shall get used to the work before the rush begins. The end of August is the slackest time in London," Lydia explained, and the next minute was vexed with herself, as Grandpapa remarked meekly: "Is it indeed, now? Thank'ee, my dear, for telling me that."

"I hope I'm going to make a success of it, and make you all proud of me," said Lydia with determination. "You know, Grandpapa, in the evenings I am going to begin writing. Do you remember that when I was quite a little girl I told you that I wanted to write books?"

"I do. You were a nice little girl, Lyddie—a sensible, well-behaved, little child. Not like those hoydens of girls at Wimbledon. If you write anything worth the postage, you may send it to me—though I'm sure I don't know who'll read it to me."

This was the nearest that Grandpapa could be induced to go towards any *rapprochement* on the eve of Lydia's departure.

She said good-bye to him as affectionately as she dared, and he replied calmly:

"Good-bye to you, my dear. Your Aunt Beryl wants me to give you a Bible or some parting advice, but I shall do nothing of the sort. If you're a good girl, you'll know how to look after yourself, and if you're a bad girl, then all the advice in the world won't keep you straight."

Lydia could not help thinking rather resentfully that Grandpapa's tones sounded just as though either contingency would leave him equally unmoved.

"Good-bye, Grandpapa—good-bye, Uncle George—down, Shamrock—good little dog!"

But Shamrock pursued Lydia and Aunt Beryl all the way to the station, and Lydia's last sight of them showed her Aunt Beryl and the station-master uniting their efforts to prevent Shamrock from taking a flying leap on to the rails.

She felt a little lonely, a very little bit frightened, as the train rushed away with her towards London.

Eighteen, which had been a really mature age while one was still at Miss Glover's, no longer seemed quite so grown up. The other people in the railway carriage all looked much older than that.

Lydia's habitual self-confidence began slightly to fail her.

What if she proved not clever enough for the work at "Elena's," and they sent her home again? Never! She would take up teaching or dressmaking in London, sooner than admit defeat. Besides, there was her writing. She thought of various fragments that she had already put on to paper, and which honestly seemed to her to be good.

The day would come, Lydia was inwardly convinced, when these would work into some not unworthy whole.

In the meanwhile, she reminded herself, in an endeavour to regain her poise of mind, that Uncle George, Aunt Beryl, Mr. Almond, the Jacksons, Miss Glover herself, had all thought her very brave and high-spirited to go away to London by herself, and had made no doubt that her courage and capabilities alike would carry her on to triumph.

She remembered also that Nathalie Palmer had written to her, in reply to her own long letter announcing her plan. She drew the envelope from her pocket, and read Nathalie's warm-hearted inquiries once more, feeling all the comfort of being so regarded by her friend.

"Lydia, I do think you're splendid," wrote Nathalie from Devonshire. "It sounds frightfully brave to be going off to live in London by yourself, and work at the accounts in a big new place like your Madame Elena's. I hope you won't be very lonely, but, of course you're sure to make friends. I do quite agree with you that it will be a tremendous *experience*, and, of course, I know experience is what you've always wanted. I wonder how soon you'll write a book. How proud I shall be when you're a famous authoress, and all your books are in rows in my bookshelf.

"Father is very interested about you. He

asked what sort of boarding-house you were going to, and I said of course Miss Raymond was frightfully particular, and it was a friend of her own. He said he was glad to hear it, and from what he remembered, you were too good-looking to be let stay just anywhere! I suppose he meant *men*!

"Remember you promised faithfully to tell me if anyone fell in love with you. I'm sure they will! No one has with me, but I hardly ever see anyone. This is the way my days are spent, mostly——"

The rest of Nathalie's letter was not so interesting, and Lydia put it away without reading further.

Her mind dwelt upon the first part of the letter, and she smiled to herself.

Even though Mr. Palmer had not seen her since she was fifteen years old, it was pleasant to know that he had thought her good-looking, and Lydia was almost certain that her appearance had improved very much since then, especially now that her dark hair was knotted up at the back of her head, with a high, Spanish-looking comb thrust into one side of the thick, outstanding twist.

"*I suppose he meant men!*"

That phrase in Nathalie's letter kept coming to her mind, and she smiled to herself a little.

It was quite time, Lydia considered, that she should learn something about men.

Grandpapa was old and didn't count—apart from the fact that, as Lydia shrewdly surmised, he was quite unlike any other man, and could never be looked upon as the representative of a type. Uncle George and Uncle Robert didn't count, either—uncles never did. Bob Senthoven Lydia dismissed with a shrug. She had not seen him since her visit to Wimbledon nearly three years ago, when he had made no favourable impression upon the young candidate for examination honours.

The only other male acquaintance to which Lydia felt that she could fairly lay claim was Mr. Monteagle Almond. She remembered her conversation with him on the subject of her departure from Regency Terrace, and the ease with which she had contrived to shift his point of view until it agreed with her own.

Judging by that solitary experience, men were not so very difficult to manage.

Lydia boldly admitted to herself that she hoped there would be men at Miss Nettleship's boarding-house.

The hope was realized.

The Bloomsbury boarding-house was large and dark, and Miss Nettleship could accommodate an almost incredible number of boarders there.

She was a brown-eyed, plaintive-looking woman, inclined to stoutness, and concealing, as Lydia afterwards discovered, considerable efficiency under a permanently distressed voice and manner.

"I hoped your auntie might have come with you," she greeted Lydia. "I could easily have put her up—we're not so very full just now, and there's always a corner. I'm so glad to see you, dear, for her sake, and I do hope you'll be happy. You must be sure and tell me if there's anything——"

The eye of the manageress was roving even as she spoke.

"Excuse me, dear—but you know what it is—one has to be on the look-out the whole time—that's the drawing-room bell, and no one answering it. I think I'll have to go myself. I know you quite understand how it is——"

Miss Nettleship hurried away, and Lydia looked round her curiously.

She was in the manageress' own office, a glass-enclosed alcove halfway up the stairs, probably originally designed for a flowery recess, in the palmy days of the old house. It was now boarded in halfway up with light-coloured grained deal, but a few sorry splinters of coloured glass still hung from the ceiling, clinking forlornly, in solitary token of the once frivolous purposes of the little alcove.

When Miss Nettleship returned, tired and apologetic, but more plaintive than ever, she showed Lydia the rest of the house.

It was built with a total disregard for domestic convenience, that Miss Nettleship assured Lydia was characteristic of old-fashioned London houses, but which she could not sufficiently deplore.

"So difficult ever to get a servant to come here, let alone *stay* here," said Miss Nettleship, sighing.

Lydia did not altogether wonder at it, when she saw the basement, occupied by kitchen, pantry, and scullery, a gas-jet permanently burning in the two latter divisions—and the only outlook of the former, rising area steps, iron railings with cracked paint, and the feet of the passers-by on the pavement.

The kitchen stairs, which led to the narrow hall, were stone, very steep, and perfectly dark.

"However they do, with the trays and all, is more than I can guess. Not that I don't carry them myself, often enough—but my heart's in my mouth the whole time. And girls are so careless, too! We had one broke her ankle, running down these stairs, not a year ago. Luckily she wasn't carrying anything but an empty tray at the time, but you never heard such a noise and a rattling in all your life! It's wicked not having the serving on the same floor as the dining-room, is what I say."

The dining-room was on the ground floor. It was a large room, with a long table already laid for dinner, running down the middle of it, and dusty aspidistras in pots stood in the bay windows, looking out, through yellowing Nottingham lace curtains, at the grimy dignity of the London plane trees on the far side of the Square railings.

Opposite the dining-room was a smoking-room, Miss Nettleship told Lydia.

"Better not look in now, perhaps," she said. "Some of the gentlemen may be in there."

"How many boarders are here now?"

"It's always varying," Miss Nettleship declared. "But I make rather a specialty, in a way, of permanent lets. There's old Miss Lillicrap—she's always here—and Mrs. Clarence, a widow, and in rather poor health—awfully badly off. And the Bulteels—husband and wife—with a boy who goes to Gower Street University. They're always here, more or less. And there's a very nice maiden lady has been here six months now, and she's said nothing about giving up her room. Miss Forster—I'm sure you'll like her, dear. She's a great card-player, and goes out a good deal. Between ourselves, she's one of the best boarders I have—very regular in settling up, and always likes the best of everything, and doesn't mind paying for it. She's always sending in fruit, and the like. It gives quite a tone to the house to see the boy leaving those baskets of fruit two or three times a week."

"Are there any girls who are going to work every day?" Lydia asked, half hoping that the reply would be in the negative.

"Not girls, no. Generally it's cheaper for girls at work to go to a woman's hostel or into rooms," said Miss Nettleship candidly. "Of course, there are one or two gentlemen. Mr. Bulteel himself has retired from business, I understand, but there's his son, Mr. Hector, that I was telling you about, and there's a Greek gentleman just now, who's only been here a week. He goes to the City every day. I'll introduce you to everyone at supper to-night, dear. It'll be strange for you at first."

Lydia was more exhilarated than alarmed. She was not shy, and it rather pleased her to think that she would be unique in her position of worker, at least amongst all the other women.

"You'd like to peep into the drawing-room," suggested Miss Nettleship, on the way up to Lydia's bedroom, and from the tone in which she spoke, Lydia guessed that this was the room of which she was proudest.

It was certainly very large and very lofty, with double folding doors in the middle, a marble fireplace at either end, and the dingy remains of much gilding still evident in the decorations.

A solitary little figure sat listlessly at one end of the room, turning over the leaves of a battered picture paper.

"Oh, good evening, Mrs. Clarence," said Miss Nettleship apologetically. "You'll excuse me disturbing you, I know. I'm just showing this young lady round. Miss Lydia Raymond—Mrs. Clarence."

The little lady stood up in an uncertain sort of way, and put out a very tiny hand to Lydia, saying nervously:

"How do you do, Miss—er—er.... I hope you're quite well."

"Quite well, thank you," said Lydia, as Aunt Beryl had taught her to say.

She despised Mrs. Clarence at sight.

The widow was very small and slight, and might have been any age between twenty-eight and thirty-nine. Her hair was of that damp, disastrous yellow, that always looks as though it had been unsuccessfully dyed, her tiny, sallow face was puckered into fretful lines, and Lydia felt convinced that she always wore just such an untidy black silk skirt, showing a sagging at the back, where it failed to meet the dingy, net blouse.

They looked at each other in silence, and Miss Nettleship said at last:

"It's quite all right, Mrs. Clarence—I knew you'd quite understand—you mustn't let us disturb you——"

She covered Lydia's retreat and her own with her usual harassed, good-natured apologies.

"Mrs. Bulteel, and Miss Forster and Mr. Hector are much more lively people than poor Mrs. Clarence," she told Lydia in a consolatory tone, on the way upstairs.

They did not pause until the top landing of all had been reached.

"This is bedroom number seventeen," optimistically declared Miss Nettleship, throwing open a door painted liver-colour, and bearing that number on it in black figures.

It looked more like a cupboard than a bedroom to Lydia, unaccustomed to London, although faint memories of lodging-hunting in her mother's days came back to her as she gazed round.

There was a combined dressing-table and chest of drawers in the room, an iron tripod for washing purposes, with enamel basin and jug, a couple of cane-seated chairs and a low iron bedstead. A print curtain, concealing a row of attenuated iron hooks and wooden pegs, hung against the wall. The only window was a fair-sized skylight.

"I'm going to send you up an easy-chair," almost whispered Miss Nettleship, looking guiltily round her, as though afraid of being overheard. "There's one in Mr. Hector Bulteel's room, and really he doesn't want it—a boy like him. There's a rocker broken, so I can get it away to have it mended, and then I'll bring it up here. This room doesn't have a rocking-chair by rights, but I know myself the comfort they are when one's been on one's feet all day. I'm determined you shall have it, and I only wish it could have been here to-day, dear—but one has to be a bit careful, and Mrs. Bulteel is so sharp, too. But it'll be quite all right—and I know you quite understand, dear."

Miss Nettleship seemed to find comfort in this assurance, which she repeated almost automatically every few moments.

Presently she left Lydia to unpack, telling her that the bell would ring for dinner at seven o'clock.

"I've put you next me at table, dear, for to-night, but of course I can't keep you there. I wish I could, but I know you understand how it is—people are so particular. So you'll understand if you're down at the end for breakfast to-morrow, won't you? Everyone takes their seat according to the time they've been here—and the latest comers down at the bottom, so you'll be next to the Greek gentleman. Shall you find your way, dear? I'd come and fetch you, but I must overlook the waitress a bit—you know how it is—one can't trust those girls a minute."

"Shall I come straight to the dining-room?"

"They generally wait for the bell in the smoking-room, but they're very prompt in. And you'd better be prompt, too, dear. That old Miss Lillicrap's *awful* for taking half of every vegetable dish that's handed, and I simply can't let them have more than enough to go once the way round."

Miss Nettleship went away, sighing.

Lydia thought that she was very kind, but talked too much.

She wondered whether Aunt Beryl had told Miss Nettleship all about her school triumphs, and the post that they had obtained for her. The thought of Aunt Beryl almost made her jump. Regency Terrace seemed such a very long way off already! She could hardly believe that she had been with them all—Grandpapa and Uncle George and Aunt Beryl, and Shamrock—at breakfast-time that very morning.

After she had taken off her hat and scrutinized herself carefully in the looking-glass, Lydia wrote to Aunt Beryl a postcard, to tell her of her safe arrival and of Miss Nettleship's kindness.

Then she went downstairs.

She could not make up her mind to open the door of the smoking-room, from behind which came the sound of feminine voices, but hung about in the narrow hall, under pretext of seeking a box in which to deposit her postcard.

Suddenly the sound of a deferential voice in her ear made her turn round.

"Did you want to post a letter?"

Lydia faced a slim, dark man, with glistening, black eyes and a clean-shaven, swarthy face. She guessed, from some indefinable intonation that hardly amounted to an accent, in his quiet, silky tones, that this was the Greek gentleman alluded to by the manageress.

"Is there a letter-box?" she asked.

"I hardly advise you to make use of it, if your card is urgent. I have seen it remain uncleared for days. The servant is very careless. But there is a pillar box just outside. Allow me!"

Lydia hesitated, but the Greek put out a slim finger and thumb, and neatly twitched the card out of her hand.

"A pleasure," said he, opening the front door.

As he left it ajar behind him, Lydia supposed that he had only a few steps to go, and remained in the hall.

In a moment he reappeared.

"That should be delivered by the first post to-morrow morning, Miss Raymond."

Lydia wondered how he knew her name, but the next minute she received enlightenment.

"I do not know the East Coast personally, but your home must be in a pleasant spot. The seaside is always attractive," conversationally observed the Greek gentleman, apparently unaware of anything obnoxious in his method of acquiring information as to his neighbour's concerns.

The reverberation of a gong saved Lydia from making any reply, although the Greek's manner was so much that of ordinary social intercourse that she almost found herself wondering whether her annoyance at his indiscretion were justified or not.

Before the sound of the gong had died away the smoking-room

door was opened, and half a dozen people had filed past Lydia into the dining-room, each one of them giving her a curious glance, sometimes accompanied by a slight bow, as they passed.

She went into the room last, and was relieved to see Miss Nettleship's broad figure and coils of untidy brown hair surmounting her pleasant, anxious-looking face, at the head of the table.

When Lydia was beside her, Miss Nettleship said aloud:

"I must introduce Miss Raymond to you. I hope she's going to be here some time. Miss Lydia Raymond, I should say. Miss Lillicrap—Mrs. Bulteel—Mr. Bulteel—Mr. Hector Bulteel—you've met Mrs. Clarence already——"

Lydia exchanged bows rather nervously right and left. Mr. Bulteel, who had a melancholy yellow face with prominent eyes, and wore an alpaca coat, and trousers that bagged at the knees, was the only person to smile at her—a doubtful, sallow sort of smile.

Lydia noticed that the Greek, although he had not been named by the manageress, also bowed, much more elaborately than anybody else, and sought her eye with a meaning look, as though some understanding already existed between them.

The meal was a very silent one.

"We quite miss Miss Forster; she's always so bright," Miss Nettleship remarked in a general sort of way. "I expect she's gone to those friends of hers again, for Bridge."

Miss Nettleship did not visibly partake of the entirety of dinner. When the tepid soup had been handed round by a particularly heavy-footed, loud-breathing servant, who never seemed to have quite enough space to move round the table without slightly lurching against the back of each chair in turn, Miss Nettleship rose and hurried away to the basement.

"I always do the carving downstairs," she told Lydia in a whisper. "Then there's no question of favouring."

Equally Miss Nettleship disappeared again after the meat course, presumably to perform the same office by the pudding.

"I'm so sorry, dear—but you know what it is—one can't trust those girls to themselves for a moment. Irene's such a feather-head, and poor old Agnes——"

Miss Nettleship squeezed past the chairs, and hurried away without particularizing the deficiencies of poor old Agnes. Nor did they require pointing out, Lydia reflected drily, if Agnes was, as she supposed, the cook.

After Miss Nettleship had left the room, the conversation, such as it was, mostly came from Mrs. Clarence and Mrs. Bulteel, a pinched, anæmic-looking little Cockney with frizzy, colourless hair.

Hector Bulteel, a yet more pallid edition of his mother, with an upstanding crest of hair that made him look like a cockatoo, said no word throughout the meal, and the Greek gentleman was equally silent.

Old Miss Lillicrap, who had her place at the right hand of the manageress, only spoke in a shrill, quavering old voice, in order to abuse the quality of her food.

Lydia looked furtively round at them all, and felt rather dismayed.

She wondered whether they would ever take on the similitude of real people to her, or if they would continue to appear as mere grotesque figures that could bear no serious relation to her new life.

VIII

THE day following Lydia's arrival in London was a Sunday and gave her further opportunity for studying her fellow-inmates.

She remained in her own room, however, most of the morning, until the maid Irene burst in upon her, a victim to that peculiar breathlessness so frequently characteristic of lodging- or boarding-house servants.

"There's a young lady wants to see you in the drawing-room," she panted.

Lydia, much surprised, went downstairs.

A strong and greasy smell of roasting pervaded the stairs, and the clatter of a Sunday dinner in preparation could be faintly heard ascending from the basement.

In the drawing-room sat old Miss Lillicrap, in a violet silk dress and a lace cap with ribbons, nodding above a newspaper.

A large, white-haired, but somehow youthful-looking female figure, unknown to Lydia, bent over the writing-table.

In the middle of the room stood Lydia's visitor, a small, plain girl, with a pale face and untidy fair hair, who put out her hand in a business-like way.

"I'm from Elena's," she said abruptly. "My name is Graham. Old Madam said I was to come and see how you were getting on, and if you'll be ready to start to-morrow."

"Oh, yes," said Lydia. "Won't you sit down?"

Miss Graham selected a chair in the middle of the room, as far as possible removed from the other two inmates.

Lydia recognized and approved the intention, but was acutely conscious that the pen of the lady at the writing-table had ceased its scratching, and that the newspaper of Miss Lillicrap was no longer rustling.

In the motionless silence of the large room Miss Graham gave Lydia information concerning the establishment of Madame Elena.

"You've seen old Madam, I know. She always interviews us girls herself before engaging us. That's one of the things that's done quite different to other places. But it's your first experience, isn't it?"

"Yes. I've only just left school."

If Lydia hoped to impress Miss Graham by the announcement, she was destined to disappointment.

"You may thank your lucky stars," said that young lady impressively, "that old Madam took to you. Girls have been tumbling over one another, by all accounts, to get that job of yours."

"Madame Ribeiro seemed very kind," said Lydia demurely.

"You won't see anything of her in the shop. Madame Elena runs that part of it altogether. She bosses the staff, of course, and does all the buying, but she's no head for figures, and that's why there's to be an accountant. You'll be sort of different from the other girls, in your position. Higher up, I mean."

Lydia felt very pleased, but she only said:

"Are all the others saleswomen?"

"Elena mostly does that herself, but she lets the senior girl, Miss Ryott, help. She and the other one, Miss Saxon, are really models. I'm at the desk."

"Do you like it?"

Miss Graham shrugged her little thin shoulders.

"I see plenty of life," she remarked. "You'll be in the show-room too. There's a table behind a screen for you, all ready. The bills will be brought to you as soon as I've stamped them."

"Shall I help in the selling?"

"You're sure to be roped in at sale-time. That's only once a year, thank God, and that was over last month. On the whole, we've got a very good berth there; I fancy quite different to shop-girls, or anything like that. You get a topping meal in the middle of the day—they say old Madam is frightfully keen on the girls being well-fed. It's a fad of hers. There's a housekeeper in the basement, an old woman called Entwhistle, and she looks after the meals. There's a first and second table for dinner."

"Are there enough of you for that?"

"Oh, yes. There are two young ladies in the millinery, and a fitter besides. And surely to goodness," said Miss Graham, "you know enough to know that the shop couldn't be left to look after itself for an hour in the middle of the day."

Lydia was not pleased at the slighting tone employed by her visitor, and replied briefly:

"I suppose not."

Then her natural instinct to engage the liking, and, if possible, the friendship of those with whom her lot might be thrown, made her exclaim frankly:

"I shan't know anything at first, I'm afraid. But I hope you'll help me a little."

"Oh," said Miss Graham matter-of-factly, "I shan't have anything much to do with you. Old Madam only sent round to say I was to come and look you up because there was nobody else. Miss Ryott is on her holiday, and won't get back till to-morrow, and Miss Saxon is a new-comer herself."

She rose, apparently indifferent to the effect of extreme ungraciousness that her speech might well have produced.

"I'd better call for you to-morrow morning. It's out of my way, but then Elena said you didn't know London, and would probably get lost. Will you be ready by half-past eight?"

"Yes," said Lydia. "I'm sorry it's out of your way."

"So am I, but it can't be helped. Whatever made you come to a place like this?" inquired Miss Graham, throwing round her a glance expressive of anything but admiration.

"The manageress is a friend of ours," Lydia said stiffly. "Do you live at home, then?"

"Lord, no. I share diggings with another girl. Well, so long then. Half-past eight to-morrow."

"I shall be waiting in the hall," said Lydia. "Good-bye, and thank you for coming."

She politely escorted Miss Graham to the front door, where the smell of cooking was stronger than ever.

As she went upstairs again, the lady of the writing-table came out of the drawing-room.

"Good morning," said she brightly. "We must introduce ourselves. I'm Miss Forster."

She laughed heartily as she spoke.

"It's nearly luncheon-time. Won't you come back into the drawing-room?"

Lydia inwardly wondered slightly why Miss Forster, who had, according to the manageress, only been in the house a few weeks, should adopt so proprietary a tone and manner, but she followed her into the drawing-room.

Miss Lillicrap had gone away, and the room was empty, as they took possession of two arm-chairs.

"We've got the place to ourselves!" proclaimed Miss Forster with some obviousness. "Most people have gone to church, but I'm a terrible pagan, I'm afraid. Now, I wonder if I'm right, Miss Raymond—but I've an idea that you're a bit of a pagan, too?"

Lydia made a civil, but meaningless, sound in reply. She had every intention of going to church in the evening with Miss Nettleship, but considered that it would appear offensive to proclaim her Christianity bluntly aloud in the face of what Miss Forster so evidently looked upon as a compliment.

She gazed at the lady, who continued to talk gaily, and instinctively drew certain conclusions from the scrutiny.

Miss Forster was a handsome, hard-faced woman, presenting a great effect of careful smartness, between forty and fifty years of age. She had obviously devoted much whalebone and a certain amount of physical force to the rigid corsetting of an over-ample figure. Her extremely white hair showed the deep, regular indentations of artificial waving, and was elaborately dressed with a good many sparkling prongs and high combs, visible even beneath the large befeathered black hat, pinned very much on to one side of her head. Her shoes were small, with Louis XV heels, and looked overtight for her short, plump feet, and her hands were carefully manicured.

Lydia uncharitably surmised that one of the effects at which she aimed was that of a woman who could have married well had she chosen to do so, and that it was to this end that she wore a sapphire and diamond ring on the third finger of her left hand, and another one with a large blue scarab on the forefinger of her right.

Her voice was high-pitched and emphatic.

"Is this your first glimpse of the world?" she demanded playfully.

Lydia felt rather at a loss for a reply.

"I've come up to work," she said at last. "But I hope I shall see something of the world while I'm here."

"Oh, I expect so. Of course, this is a quiet part of town—not like Kensington or the West End, by any means—in fact, I've never lived so far out before. My friends are always trying to get me to move into a little West End flat somewhere, but I say, 'No; I don't care for the bother of housekeeping.' And really we're quite well done here, you know, and of course I don't hesitate to order in any little extra thing. I'm afraid I like my comforts, Miss Raymond. It's what I've been accustomed to all my life."

"Have you always lived in London?" Lydia politely inquired.

She was remembering Grandpapa's axiom: *Always let the other people talk about themselves.*

It appeared that Miss Forster did not require much encouragement to do so with great animation, and a number of rather superfluous gesticulations, illustrative of her words.

"Oh, my dear Miss Raymond! I always say I'm a rolling stone!"

Miss Forster's hands described rapid revolutions one over the other in the air.

"I've been in all sorts of places, but I've come to the conclusion that London is the place to live in. There's always something to *do* there. If it's bad weather, there are concerts or theatres always going on—and one can always pop round to one's club and get a game of Bridge."

As Miss Forster enumerated these resources of urban life, she successively agitated her fingers up and down an imaginary keyboard, gazed eagerly through imaginary opera-glasses held up to her eyes, and rapidly dealt out a few imaginary cards.

"I'm a tremendous gambler, I'm afraid. I love my game of Bridge. There are some dear friends of mine living in Lexham Gardens, who frequently give Bridge parties. I daresay you've heard of them—Sir Rupert and Lady Honoret?"

"I don't think I have."

"No?" said Miss Forster, looking rather disappointed. "She's so very well known in Society that I thought you might have. I must introduce you some day. Such a clever woman!"

Suddenly an echo came back to Lydia's well-trained memory. She was in the drawing-room of the Wimbledon house again, listening to Aunt Evelyn's droning voice reading from her illustrated paper:

"Fancy! it says here that 'the wife of this city magnate is no mean critic of *l'école moderne*, having herself contributed on several occasions to the sum of New Thought literature, in the shape of several charmingly written sketches *pour nos autres*.' That would be this Sir Rupert Honoret's wife, I suppose. They say she's a Jewess."

"Doesn't Lady Honoret write?" said Lydia.

"That's it!" cried Miss Forster delightedly. "I thought you must have heard of her; she's *so* well known."

"Yes, I have heard of her. I remember now," said Lydia, inwardly congratulating herself on the excellence of her memory.

"I feel certain that you and I are going to be pals," Miss Forster exclaimed breezily. "Between ourselves, there's nobody I've taken to very violently here. I really thought it was more of a residential hotel than a boarding-house, or I shouldn't have come. One really can't entertain one's friends here, with such awful servants, and that terrible old Miss Lillicrap always about the place. She has a heart, you know, so one can't say much."

Both Miss Forster's hands flew to her ample bust, in indication of the nature of Miss Lillicrap's complaint.

"However, I belong to a *very* smart West End Ladies' Club, so I can always give my little card parties there. You must come and have tea there some day," said Miss Forster airily.

"I should like to," replied Lydia truthfully. She was not attracted by Miss Forster, but people with literary ladyships for their friends might be very useful, and Lydia quite complacently told herself that the accident of her having listened to, and remembered, Aunt Evelyn's item of information, had done her good service with this woman, who might easily bring her into that world where she most wished to find herself.

She began to think that, perhaps, after all, the boarding-house might count for even more than Madame Elena's.

At dinner, which on Sundays was in the middle of the day, the Greek, who was her neighbour, talked to her and asked if she were going out in the afternoon.

"I have to unpack," said Lydia demurely.

She had unpacked almost everything in the course of the morning, but she thought that the Greek meant to ask if she would go out with him, and instinct told her that his evident admiration would only be increased by a pretence at coyness.

"Do you care for the theatre?" he inquired next.

"Oh, I love it," said Lydia frankly.

"We must make up a party one evening. Mrs. Bulteel is very fond of a good show, I know," said the Greek.

Lydia felt excited.

Evidently her life was not to be all hard work.

She ventured into the drawing-room after the hot and heavy meal, but found that Sunday afternoon was by common consent given up to repose.

Miss Lillicrap and Miss Forster both went to their rooms, little Mrs. Clarence, sunk into an arm-chair with a library novel, fell asleep at once, and snored faintly from time to time; Mrs. Bulteel disposed herself elegantly upon the drawing-room sofa, and said to Lydia:

"I hope you don't mind me having my toes up like this?"

"Oh, no, indeed."

"I'm not very strong. My husband and my son go for a walk on Sunday afternoons, but I'm not very strong."

Mrs. Bulteel closed her eyes complacently, and also went to sleep.

Lydia took her fountain-pen from her pocket, having first sampled the pens on the writing-table, and found them all very old, rather rusty, and either broken or cross-nibbed, and wrote a letter to Aunt Beryl. She gave full details of Miss Nettleship's good-nature, and of her visit from Miss Graham, and even reported a little of her conversation with Miss Forster, the friend of Sir Rupert and Lady Honoret. She said nothing at all about the Greek gentleman.

The evening meal, at seven o'clock on week-days, was not until half-past eight on Sundays, and Miss Nettleship, after entertaining Lydia to tea in her own room, took her to church at six o'clock, talking all the way.

Lydia was bored, and in church began to feel rather homesick and apprehensive of her first day's work on the morrow.

Supper proved to be a cheerless meal. There was no soup, only portions of cold pressed beef and beetroot, and a chilly helping of custard-pudding upon each plate. The cheese was substantial enough, but the section of the dish that held biscuits was empty by the time it reached Lydia, and although she asked Irene for some bread, Irene forgot to bring it.

She went to bed still feeling hungry.

Next morning she was introduced to the establishment of Madame Elena.

"Us girls have to use the side door, of course," Miss Graham explained. But before they went inside she showed Lydia the front entrance, with "Elena" scrawled in gilt letters above the door, and a small, diamond-paned window that displayed only a gilt chair, over which was flung a brilliant scarlet and gold kimono, and a little gilt stand, on which hung a necklace of green jade, surmounted by a minute hat composed entirely of fluted purple tulle, apparently held together by a jewelled buckle.

"Madame Elena dressed the window herself," said Miss Graham. "She goes in for colour contrasts."

Her tone denoted no particular admiration, but Lydia privately was a good deal impressed by the window. Not with this wonderfully effective restraint were the shop fronts decked into which she had hitherto been accustomed to gaze.

She expected Madame Elena to be an æsthetic-looking creature in an artistic smock, and was disappointed at the sight of a very fat, good-natured-faced woman, with an immense mop of auburn hair and a heavily-powdered face. Instead of the art-smock, she wore a tight black skirt, that seemed to emphasize the disproportionate shortness of her legs, and a lace shirt with an elaborate high collar and falling *jabot* of lace.

"Brought a black dress?" she inquired. "Rosie here will show you where the girls' dressing-room is, and where you can leave your things. You change here, of course. What about shoes and stockings?"

She shook her head at Lydia's black Oxford shoes.

"Get a pair of court slippers at lunch-time. Rosie will tell you where to go. Stockings don't matter, as you'll be behind your desk all the time. You needn't worry about corsets, either, not being a model. Now go and change, then you can come back to me here, and we'll go through the books together and give you some idea of your job."

"Are you nervous?" Rosie Graham asked Lydia with a quick look, when they were in the basement dressing-room.

"Oh, no, not really," Lydia replied, with more spirit than accuracy.

Miss Graham burst into an impish laugh.

"Oh, you lovely little liar!" said she.

Lydia was not sure whether to admit the truth of the apostrophe or not.

She used all her intelligence during the next three hours, but Madame Elena's method of instruction was slap-dash and sketchy, and Lydia learnt most during the frequent intervals when her teacher was called away, and she was left alone with the great ledgers and invoice-books.

The technical terms, and the abbreviations especially, puzzled her greatly, but much of the work reminded her of the old problems at Miss Glover's, when she had been told to "show the working" on the black-board for the benefit of the other girls.

The stock appeared to consist of evening gowns, millinery and an occasional scarf or veil. Nothing was made on the premises except hats, but Madame Elena sometimes undertook commissions, for very favoured customers, during her trips to Paris.

Some of the papers relating to wholesale purchases were in French, and Lydia regretfully felt that her old deficiency would find her out again.

In spite of the French, however, she thought that the book-keeping would prove to be well within her capacity, and felt cheered.

Madame Elena was very good-natured, not at all the overbearing and dictatorial principal that Lydia had half expected to find her. They worked together in her room all the morning, Lydia uninterruptedly, and Madame Elena in the midst of many respectful summonses and urgent telephone calls.

Just before one o'clock, a tall girl with dark hair, dressed in the saleswoman's austerely smart black and white, once more announced the arrival of an important client.

Madame Elena darted through into the shop again, and this time was away for nearly an hour.

Through the door of her tiny office, which she had left ajar, Lydia could hear an occasional phrase:

"I really don't think you'd ever regret it ... it's so *exactly* your style. I really shouldn't urge it if I didn't think you'd be pleased with it.... Oh, *no*, Moddam—you couldn't call that *cerise* by any possibility. Old rose it is—just your shade...."

Madame Elena came back at last, flinging herself into the chair before the writing-table.

"Oof! I thought we should never get done. She meant to take it, all the time, too. Now, Miss Raymond, let's see you enter that. Here's the bill."

"Motor-bonnet, at seventy-five and sixpence," Lydia read.

"You must describe it in your entry, so that we shall recognize it," Madame Elena declared. "Turn up the invoice."

When Lydia had found it she discovered with surprise that the recent purchase figured as "Rose-red and ash-grey motoring capote."

"*That* sounds more like it!" said the principal, in satisfied accents. "Now you'll know how it should go down on the account."

She pulled out a gold watch from her tight waist-band.

"Poor child! the girls will have finished dinner. I suppose they didn't like to fetch you while you were in here—and quite right too. You'd better come out and get some lunch with me."

They went out through the show-room, and Lydia saw Rosie Graham sitting in the small, glass-panelled box near the door, with neat piles of change on the ledge in front of her.

As they went past, Lydia meekly walking behind Madame Elena, Rosie made a derisive face at her, and Lydia understood that it was an unusual honour to be taken out to lunch by the principal.

They went to a small restaurant close by, and Madame Elena made Lydia blush by remarking impressively to the waitress who brought them the bill of fare:

"Make out two separate bills for this, waitress. Now, my dear, what are you going to have?"

Lydia had not expected to be Madame Elena's guest at the meal, but she considered the emphasis indelicate, and wished that it had not been thought necessary.

On the whole, however, she liked Madame Elena, who kept up

an incessant stream of lively talk, and gave her a quantity of information about the business, the customers and the staff.

"That little Graham, now—she's been with us ever since we opened, and done her job first class. But she'll never do any better for herself than she's doing now. The reason why, because she's got no tact. I'd never trust her to show so much as a motor-veil to a client—she'd tell her the colour was too young for her, as soon as winking. Of course, my dear, I'm telling you these things because you're not quite in the same position as the show-room girls. That's an understood thing, and has been from the first. More like my understudy you'll come to be in time, I hope. That is if you and I understand one another, as I think we're going to."

Lydia felt flattered.

"I'll do my very best," she said earnestly.

"I'm sure you will, and once you've mastered the system you'll be all right, and I'm sure I shall be thankful to get the books off my mind. I've no head for figures, and never had," said Madame Elena, with perfect complacency.

She dismissed Lydia at five o'clock, although the working day was not over until six.

"But I know well enough what a first day's work is," she remarked shrewdly. "You've a splitting head, and don't know a one from a two by this time. Trot along, and if I were you, I'd walk home. The air will do you good. You can start properly to-morrow. It's a slack time of year, anyhow."

Lydia departed gratefully.

Business life was not going to be the inhuman affair that books represented it to be, after all; Madame Elena had been good-natured and patient, although Lydia easily divined that she could be far otherwise on occasion, and although she had had no opportunity for intercourse with the other girls, they had looked at her in a not unfriendly way.

She walked across the Park, gazing with interest at the people she met, until she perceived that several of the men that passed her were inclined to stare frankly back at her, or to smile furtively.

Lydia remembered certain pieces of advice given long ago by Aunt Beryl, and which had always been disregarded, because they sounded so singularly superfluous to the quiet neighbourhood of Regency Terrace.

She ceased to look about her, and walked more quickly, conscious all the time of a certain exultation.

Surely men only stared like that at pretty girls or attractive girls?

She wished that she knew whether she were really pretty or not.

In a very little while Lydia lost the sense of novelty, and began to feel as though she had always been independent.

She soon found that her life at Madame Elena's and her life at the boarding-house had both become quite real to her, and very interesting. Each was absolutely separate from the other, but both made up a sum of experiences that absorbed and excited her.

People were extraordinarily interesting.

For all her capability and astonishing effect of maturity, Lydia was not quite nineteen years old, and it was only much later on that she realized how entirely her interest in her fellow-creatures had confined itself to the effect produced upon them by the personality of Lydia Raymond.

IX

THERE were wheels within wheels at Madame Elena's establishment. Romantic friendships for one another amongst Madame Elena's "young ladies," sudden desperate quarrels and equally desperate reconciliations, all formed part of the fabric of everyday life, and afforded discussion at the midday dinner in the basement.

The girls, as Miss Graham had said, were all catered for.

"Don't be afraid to come again," Mrs. Entwhistle, the housekeeper, would exclaim jovially from the head of the table, acting, it was understood, under direct orders from Madame Ribeiro, whom the girls called Old Madam.

It was well known that Old Madam would not have anyone who might be working at Elena's stinted of a good meat meal in the middle of the day, which she called "an economy in the end." The number of helpings was never restricted, and the meat was always followed by a substantial pudding.

Lydia at first watched with amazement the two accomplished young women from the millinery, both of them pale London girls, send up their plates twice or three times, in eager response to Mrs. Entwhistle's invitation.

Miss Graham, always at her desk, and the little needlewoman who attended to alterations, were the only girls on the premises not selected, partly on account of good looks.

"A pretty saleswoman sets off the goods," was another of Old Madam's reported aphorisms. "Prettiness" was the keynote of the establishment, and with this end in view, Christian names were always used in business hours.

Rosie Graham told Lydia that Miss Ryott's name, Georgina, not considered an ornamental one by Madame Elena, had been abbreviated to Gina, as having a pleasant *soupçon* of Italian romance. Gina, in fact, rather looked the part. She was a tall girl, of a full figure, with crape-black hair rolled back from a round, cream-coloured face, dark-brown eyes and beautiful teeth.

Gina only painted her lips a very little.

Miss Saxon, the other show-room "young lady" on the other hand, who said that her name was Marguerite, painted her face, as well as her lips, most artistically. She was flaxen-haired and very slim, with babyish blue eyes and a tiny mouth. She was always called for by Madame Elena to show off any *toilette de jeune fille*.

Lydia found it easy to believe that the staff was made up of young women taken from a class superior to that of the ordinary London shop-girl. That was Old Madam's policy.

At intervals, Madame Ribeiro, always unannounced, drove up to the shop entrance of "Elena's," in her little old-fashioned, closed carriage, and walked slowly through the show-room, up the shallow steps that led to millinery, and into the small alcove, glass-panelled, where sat Madame Elena, poring over large tomes, or sometimes inditing scrawled communications on large, mauve-coloured sheets of notepaper, with "Elena" carelessly running across the top corner of the page in big purple lettering.

Old Madam never distinguished Lydia by any special notice on these occasions. She generally remained with Madame Elena for half an hour or so, and sometimes the latter would strike her little bronze bell, and ask, "Marguerite, *chérie*" or "Gina, my child" to bring in afternoon tea for Madam.

"Anyone would think we were tea-shop girls," said Miss Ryott pettishly.

The order meant an excursion to the basement, where Mrs. Entwhistle had to be found, the keys asked for, and bread-and-butter cut very thin and arranged on a china plate, and two or three sponge biscuits taken out of a special tin, and the whole arranged on a small green-and-white tea-service consecrated to Madame Elena's use. But then Madame Elena had her tea sent up at a reasonable hour, when the girls had theirs, and Mrs. Entwhistle prepared it, which she would never do unaided at any hour earlier than four o'clock. If Old Madam chose to have tea before half-past three one of the girls must get it ready.

Gina, especially on a hot afternoon in the slack season, very much preferred the shop.

"Shall I help you, dear?" affectionately inquired Marguerite. "Lydia could give us a call if anyone came in. Not that anyone will—they are all in Scotland or at the sea somewhere—lucky things!"

"Thanks, dear—how sweet of you!"

They went away arm-in-arm, leaving Lydia drowsily writing out "Marked down" tickets, copied from a list of Madame Elena's making.

"*That* friendship won't last," remarked Miss Graham sapiently, from her desk.

She was right, as usual.

Lydia had not been very long at Elena's when the Great Quarrel took place, and assumed an intensity that could only have obtained during the month of September.

It all reminded Lydia very much of the girls at Miss Glover's school.

Gina, it was evident enough, had hitherto dominated the little group of girls, but her temporary infatuation for the society of Miss Marguerite Saxon had rather diminished her prestige, and Marguerite, moreover, had made herself popular with the millinery young ladies by talking agreeably to them at dinner-time, when they sat together at the second table. Consequently they championed her with vigour.

"It really is too bad, you know, dear. Marguerite is awfully sensitive—those blondes so often are, much more so than brunettes, I fancy—and of course she feels it all the more because they used to be such *friends*. That's what hurts her so much."

"Well, Gina is hurt about it, too—and has cause to be, in my opinion," inexorably said the girl who did alterations.

The first and second tables were allowed to overlap during the slack season very often.

"How did it begin?" Lydia asked.

But to this there was no satisfactory reply.

How did the slackening of those romantic bonds first make itself felt?

"Marguerite couldn't help noticing that Gina's manner had altered, of course," said someone vaguely.

From this painful illumination it appeared as though Miss Saxon and Miss Ryott had proceeded to revive their drooping interest in one another by a series of mutual provocations.

"Gina is awfully proud. You couldn't expect her to take the first step. I mean, she's so frightfully proud."

"You know, I believe Madame Elena knows about it," said Rosie, giggling, precluded by Mrs. Entwhistle's presence from making use of the auburn-headed principal's usual *sobriquet* of "Old Peroxide."

It was quite true that Madame Elena was inclined to favour Gina. Lydia had noticed it with resentment.

When Rosie Graham's shrewdness was justified, as it almost invariably was, by the event, and Madame Elena showed definite signs of partisanship in the quarrel, Gina became established as the heroine of the hour.

One afternoon, just before closing time, she suddenly burst into tears after a prolonged search for a mislaid pencil—that eternal preoccupation of the shop-girl's day.

"Don't cry," said Lydia very gently, and feeling very impatient, since she disliked any display of emotion in other people—unless it was directly concerned with herself.

"I'll lend you mine."

Such a loan was unheard of, for the pencils, suspended by a chain from each girl's waist, were in constant use, and the rule obliged each one to provide her own.

"Oh, I don't care," sobbed Gina, recklessly noisy. "Thanks most awfully, dear. I know it's sweet of you—but I'm fed up with everything."

She sank into a chair, still sobbing hysterically.

"So are we all," said Miss Saxon low and viciously, looking up from the drawer before which she was kneeling, carefully swathing some frail chiffon scarves in tissue-paper. "So are we all, I should imagine, in this heat and all, but we don't make a song and dance about it, I suppose. What *I* should call absolute carrying on for notice."

As though to verify the words, Madame Elena's glass door flew open.

"What's all this noise?" she asked irately. "If you girls think you're here to make a row——"

Her eye fell on Gina, who had the wisdom to make a visible effort to check her sobs and rise to her feet. Lydia noted, with instinctive approval, that the face she turned to her principal was paler than usual, with black marks under either eye.

"I'm very sorry, I'm sure," she faltered.

"What's the matter?"

Gina was silent, gulping.

Madame Elena looked sharply round. Her eye fell on Marguerite, still demurely smoothing out silver paper.

Miss Saxon, less intelligent than Gina, and evidently far less intuitive than the watching Lydia, made the mistake of allowing a very small sneer to show itself upon her little roseleaf face.

Lydia saw Madame Elena's expression alter.

She laid an authoritative hand upon Gina's shoulder, and gave her a friendly push.

"Go in there," she said. "I'm going to get to the bottom of this."

They vanished into the principal's own sanctum, Marguerite, apparently no expert in the interpretation of signs, observing with satisfaction:

"I hope she'll get properly skinned alive for making a row like that in business hours. Why, it's downright unladylike."

Miss Graham, from her desk in the corner, gave her little scoffing laugh.

"Don't be a fool, Marguerite. She was playing for that, of course. She made that noise on purpose so as Perox should hear her, and ask what was up. Old Perox has been dying to hear what the row's about between you two for days, and now Gina can pitch her own yarn. Just like Gina!"

Lydia was astounded, as she often was, at the little Cockney's penetration.

"Why are you staring, goggle-eyes?" said Miss Graham, rudely but not unkindly. "Don't you think it's true?"

With Marguerite Saxon's small, squirrel face turned to catch her answer, Lydia made a diplomatic evasion.

"Rather an unfair advantage to take, wasn't it?" she hazarded.

"I'll tell Gina you think so," said Rosie, like a shot.

She burst out laughing at the dismay which Lydia, involuntarily, and to her own vexation, felt that she reflected upon her face.

"You don't like that, do you?" remarked the terrible Miss Graham. "You want to run with the hare and hunt with the hounds—keep in with everyone all round, and boss the lot of us. I know your sort. I daresay you'll bring it off, too, given you're here long enough."

"I don't know what you mean," said Lydia, instinctively adopting the phraseology of her surroundings.

Rosie gave her little shrug.

"Don't you worry, I'm only chaffing. *I* shan't make mischief. I like pulling your leg," explained Miss Graham kindly, "because it's so dead easy, that's all."

"Don't mind her, dear," said Marguerite. "That's her style, that is. It doesn't mean anything. I say, do *hark* at that girl in there!"

Faint sounds, as of an eloquent outpouring of words mingled with an occasional sob, came from the partition behind which Gina and the principal were secluded.

"She's crying dreadfully," said Lydia, with a dim idea of diminishing, by her compassionate tone, the effect of her previous comment upon Miss Ryott's methods.

A sardonic glance from Rosie Graham made her uneasily aware that this manœuvre had been only too transparent.

However, Rosie only remarked scornfully:

"Crying! That's nothing at the end of a day's work. Anyone can cry in the evenings—in fact, it's easier than not. One's tired, and it's been beastly hot all day, and it's a relief to sit down and howl. Most girls do it regularly if they aren't going out anywhere, and can risk having a red nose. Wait till you see a girl crying at eight o'clock in the morning—then it's time enough to be sorry for her. If she cries then, it's because she can't help it. If she cries at night she's just letting herself go."

"*My* difficulty is that I never can cry, however much I feel things," said Miss Saxon, true to the feminine instinct, so much condemned by Lydia's grandfather, of making instant personal application of a generality.

"I get awfully upset—quite foolishly so, mother always says. 'You'll never go through life, dear,' she says, 'if you take every little thing to heart so much.' It's awfully wearing, too—things kind of prey on me. I just go on turning them over and over in my own mind, you know. But as for crying—well, it's just as though I couldn't. I'd give anything to, sometimes—you know, I feel it would be such a relief, like—but I never was one to cry, even as a child."

Miss Saxon, much interested in her own monologue, appeared as though she might go on for ever.

Rosie Graham made an expressive grimace at Lydia, and formed with her lips:

"Good reason why!" at the same time pointing to her own little sallow face, with a glance at Marguerite's carefully rose-tinted cheeks.

Lydia smiled discreetly, safely conscious that she had her back turned to Miss Saxon.

The opportunity for which she had been looking came that evening.

She waited for Gina.

The other girls went down to the dressing-room, pinned on their straw and flower-wreathed hats, took hasty glances into the tiny mirror propped up against the window, and rubbed at their shining, heated faces with leaves of *papier poudre*, torn from little pink or blue books. Only Marguerite Saxon possessed a small silver elegance, hanging from a long chain, containing a little puff, with which she dabbed the tip of her nose delicately.

"Good night, dear," she said cordially to Lydia, who responded as cordially, with her readiest smile. Already she guessed that Miss Saxon was willing to make a bid for her friendship, in the new-born apprehension that the tide of partisanship was turning rapidly in Gina's favour.

With Gina, the advance was even easier. It was long after closing hours when she finally emerged from Madame Elena's room, and then she was not alone. Madame Elena, in the immense be-plumed hat and long suède gloves that she always affected, preceded her.

"Lydia! What are you doing here?" she exclaimed sharply.

"I've finished those Paris model tickets, Madame Elena," said Lydia meekly.

She had printed over two dozen cards whilst she waited, it being one of the sign manuals of the establishment to display all such tickets in elaborate fancy letterings.

"You haven't!"

Madame Elena made one of her rapid, swooping movements, and snatched up a handful of the cards, miraculously avoiding those on which the ink was still wet.

"Now I call that charming," said Madame Elena, with genuine enthusiasm. "First class. How on earth did you manage to get the letters all different and so straight! But don't stay overtime another evening like that. You may find yourself locked in."

She nodded and passed out of the side door, demonstratively waiting for the two girls, in order to lock it behind her.

"I get in here," she said, pausing where a long row of omnibuses was drawn up beside the kerb. "Good night, girls."

"Good night, Madame Elena," they chorussed politely.

"Which is your way, dear?" inquired Gina, who called everyone "dear" without discrimination.

"Right across the Park. I generally walk," said Lydia.

"Rotten to be so far off. *I* live miles out, too, right the way to Mornington Crescent. I'll walk with you, if you like. The air'll do my head good, and I may as well get in at Oxford Circus as anywhere else."

"Have you a headache?" said Lydia sympathetically.

"I should think I have! Why, I've been howling, on and off, since five o'clock. I daresay you think I'm a fool," said Gina dolorously.

"No, of course I don't. I'm so sorry for you."

"Thanks, dear. I don't generally say much about things when I feel them," said Miss Ryott pensively, "but I don't mind talking to you, between ourselves, like. Now, Rosie Graham—she's the sarcastic sort—or tries to be. I could never let myself go in front of that girl——"

Gina paused, expressively enough, in lieu of seeking in the barren fields of the shop-girl's range of imagery.

"I know what you mean," said Lydia. She had long ago found out the incalculable value of this sympathetic, and entirely non-committal, form of words.

"You may have noticed that I haven't been exactly what you might call a Sunny Jim lately," said Miss Ryott.

She looked sidelong at Lydia, who turned a deeply interested gaze upon her, but said nothing at all. The echo of Grandpapa's wisdom came back to her, as it so often did: "Always let the other people talk about themselves." And once more it was justified.

Whilst her companion talked, Lydia congratulated herself upon the success of her manœuvre in waiting for Gina, and at the same time impressing upon Madame Elena, ever alert for signs of enthusiasm in the staff, her eager devotion to her work. There was not another employee in the shop who would voluntarily have remained on after hours, apparently from utter absorption in the task on hand.

Lydia marvelled, with perfectly genuine wonder, that none of them should have the wit to see how enormously worth while it was to sacrifice an hour or two of leisure once in a way for the sake of the immense effect that such a display produced upon the authorities.

She never made the mistake of attempting to deceive herself as to her own motives, and was consequently able to estimate to the full the results at which she had consciously aimed.

"You're a perfect dear to have listened to me," said Gina warmly when they parted. "I'm sure I've been the most frightful bore, really."

Lydia assured her that this had not been the case, and was able to do so with the more earnestness that she was inwardly full of exhilaration at the growing conviction that her personality was once more giving her prominence amongst her surroundings.

The next day Marguerite Saxon twice emphatically called her "my dear"—a mark of potential friendship as distinguished from the professional and abstracted "dear," that invariably punctuated the day's intercourse.

She was also required to listen, during the tea-interval, to Miss Saxon's version of the recent disturbance.

It need scarcely be said that Lydia's perfectly non-committal sympathy was extended as freely to Marguerite as it had been to Gina, with the result that each declared a warm liking for her, and she speedily became the central figure in their little world.

Madame Elena was not prone to personal enthusiasms, and the signs that she gave of having distinguished Lydia from among her compeers, were all but imperceptible. Only Lydia's ruthless clear-sightedness where her own interests were concerned enabled her to discern them.

She soon found that the two young ladies in the millinery were rather looked down upon by the show-room young ladies, who had, indeed, little opportunity for intercourse with them. Nevertheless, Lydia smiled sedulously at them when she said, "Good morning," and never pretended deafness when one or the other of them asked her to "pass along the bread, please," at dinner.

Consequently they were overheard to say to one another that Miss Raymond was the only lady in the place, so far as manners went.

Mrs. Entwhistle was somewhat of the same opinion, since Lydia was the only girl who never grumbled at helping her when Old Madam's unexpected calls led to a sudden demand for afternoon tea.

There remained Miss Rosie Graham.

Lydia was perhaps more nearly afraid of her than she had ever been of any member of her own sex.

To a Cockney sharpness of tongue, Rosie added an almost un-canny power of insight into the minds of her neighbours, and it was commonly asserted amongst the girls that she could "thought-read."

The "thought-reading," Lydia decided, was a trick, based upon natural shrewdness and an almost infallible instinct for the detection of small affectations and insincerities, but it may reasonably be sup-posed that it added no sense of security to the circles of which Miss Graham was a member.

Lydia knew that Rosie was not, and never would be, popular, but she uneasily surmised in her a strength of character that might equal, if it did not surpass, her own. And the idea was disturbing to Lydia's conception of her own allotted rôle in life, well to the forefront of the stage.

She was always charming to Miss Graham, in accordance with her invariable rule, but after three months at Madame Elena's she was still vexedly aware that the medium by which the charm could be made efficacious had yet to be discovered.

It was obviously waste of time to say to Rosie, as she might have said to Marguerite Saxon, for instance:

"You do look tired to-day. I'm sure you're not a bit strong."

For, whereas Miss Saxon would have denied the charge, simper-ing with gratification the while, and at an early opportunity have returned the kindness by some such compliment as, "What a sweet figure that costume gives you, dear. I'm sure you wear lovely corsets," it might safely be assumed that Rosie would shrug her shoulders, and retort matter-of-factly that her pallor was due to indigestion. She frankly disliked personalities, although she was willing enough to give her opinion, uncivilly and often unkindly, although never maliciously, in regard to other people.

Lydia sometimes thought that the only avenue of approach lay in the sense of humour that they shared, and which was deficient in the other members of the small group. And it always gave her an odd sense of reassurance when, in the course of the day, some trivial incident, or chance word, would cause her eyes and those of Rosie Graham to meet, involuntarily and quite instinctively, in a silent laugh.

X

"THERE'S only one piece each," said old Miss Lillicrap, in the sharp, fierce squeak that the other boarders always heard with dismayed resentment, rendered powerless because of her extreme age, and the violet tinge that shadowed her hard old lips.

Miss Lillicrap had been known to have a violent and mysterious "attack" for a less reason than the appropriation of a second piece of seed-cake at tea-time on a Sunday afternoon by someone other than herself.

The boarders assembled in the drawing-room instantly entered into the unanimous league of a silent resolution to ignore Miss Lillicrap's indelicate insistence on the extremely limited quantity of cake supplied by Miss Nettleship.

"Meal-time again!" sighed little Mrs. Clarence, at the same time edging her chair forward, so as to sit nearest to the small milk-jug and inadequately-filled sugar-basin. "It always seems to be time to eat, somehow." Her pale, pink-rimmed blue eyes were anxiously scanning the food on the table as she spoke.

"Only one piece each," snapped Miss Lillicrap again, more loudly than before.

Again they all ignored her.

"Who's going to do 'mother,' and pour out?" asked Mrs. Bulteel with a rather nervous laugh.

Everyone knew that as the principal married woman in the room, she felt herself entitled to the office of dignity. Almost equally well, everyone knew that it would be disputed.

"I thought Miss Forster did that," said old Miss Lillicrap.

Had Miss Forster been present she would certainly have supported Mrs. Bulteel.

"Miss Forster is out, Miss Lillicrap," retorted Mrs. Bulteel, raising her already shrill voice, so as to impress upon Miss Lillicrap that she was old, and must therefore be very deaf as well.

"Oh, all right—all right. Yesterday I was awake nearly all night, the tea was so strong."

"I'll give you the first cup," shrilled Mrs. Bulteel, provided with an excellent excuse for snatching the tea-pot before Mrs. Clarence, who, as a widow, could have no status at all, could put her little be-ringed, claw-like fingers round the handle.

Lydia, who, for reasons connected with her own undoubted popularity at the boarding-house, never took part in the tea-time amenities of the boarders—of which, indeed, she was only witness on occasional Saturday and Sunday afternoons—looked sympathetically at Mr. Bulteel, waiting nervously for the teacups which he habitually handed politely round.

He evidently thought his wife very spirited and clever when she used her shrewish Cockney tongue against the other women.

"Allow me," said he, taking round the cups of strong, black brew. He threw a resentful glance, as he did so, at the Greek gentleman, who never took his share in dispensing these small courtesies. He only stood, as he usually did, in front of the empty fireplace, his hands in his pockets, and his dark eyes roaming sardonically round the room. He was still spoken of as "the Greek gentleman," since no one had mastered his name. Lydia had listened with interest to various conversations about him, but had derived little information from them. It might be entertaining, but it was not particularly illuminating to hear Mrs. Bulteel say to Mrs. Clarence, as Lydia had heard her say a little while ago, in a very penetrating manner:

"That's not a face I should *trust*."

Mrs. Clarence, who never ventured to differ from anybody, and least of all from Mrs. Bulteel, who had a live husband and son to testify to the fact that she had justified her feminine existence, had only replied doubtfully:

"No? Well, perhaps you're right. What makes you think...?"

"He looks as though he had foreign blood in him." Mrs. Bulteel adduced the damning grounds for her inference with gloomy prescience, which she appeared to think amply justified by the facts that the Greek spoke English with a slight accent, and had a name that even Miss Nettleship only rendered as Mr. M ... m ... m.

A little while afterwards the unconquerable Mrs. Bulteel had actually asked him outright, "And do tell me, *how* is your name pronounced?" in a very intelligent way, as though she knew of two or three excellent alternatives.

To which the Greek gentleman had replied, with slightly outspread, olive fingers:

"Just—exactly—as you please."

"But how do *you* say it in your own country?"

"I am not in my own country."

"I know that. You are a foreigner," said Mrs. Bulteel, much as she might have said, "You are a cannibal." "But if you *were* in your own country?"

Then had replied the Greek gentleman morosely:

"I should have no need to say it at all. It is too well known."

And Mrs. Bulteel, seeing herself defeated, could only cry out in a shaking voice the time-honoured indictment of the English middle classes of whatever is slightly less than blatantly obvious:

"Oh! How sarcastic!"

Nothing could be more evident than that the Greek was indifferent to the charge, or, indeed, to any other that might be proffered against him by his fellow-inmates.

That very Sunday morning had been spent by him in reading a French novel in the drawing-room, whilst almost all the other inmates had decorously attended church.

"Will you keep some tea for Hector?" suggested Mr. Bulteel, as his wife put down the tea-pot and uncrooked her little finger.

"I have come to an arrangement with the manageress about Hector's tea," retorted Mrs. Bulteel, with a magnificence that seemed inadequate to the cup of strong tea, and slices of bread-and-butter on a thick plate now probably waiting on the kitchen range for Hector's return.

"The poor boy is never much later than half-past five, after all, even on week-days."

Mrs. Clarence and Miss Lillicrap exchanged a look. Everyone knew that the main interest of the senior members of the Bulteel *ménage* was to exercise a rigorous censorship over every unaccounted-for moment of their only son's existence.

It was as a matter of course that everyone present heard the accustomed routine of question and answer gone through by Hector and his parents on the youth's entrance into the drawing-room.

"Is that you, Hector?" said Mrs. Bulteel mildly, as soon as her son had slouched to a seat, and no further doubt of his identity could possibly prevail.

"Have you asked for your tea?" Mr. Bulteel inquired.

"The girl opened the door to me."

Few of the boarders possessed latch-keys, and Hector was not one of these.

"That girl!" exclaimed his mother. "Better ring, and I'll tell her."

Mrs. Clarence looked rather awed. She would never have dared to ring the drawing-room bell for the parlour-maid.

Lydia herself had come in late for tea, and although Mr. Bulteel had handed her a cup, smiling rather apologetically, there was very little left to eat.

"There's no more cake—nothing left!" cried old Miss Lillicrap with a sort of vicious triumph, as Lydia gazed at the empty plates on the table.

Lydia shrugged her shoulders, and Mr. Bulteel said nervously and kindly:

"They will bring you some more, no doubt."

Everybody knew that any such concession to a late arrival was most unlikely, and the effect produced was proportionate when the Greek gentleman, on the arrival of Hector Bulteel's belated cup and saucer, turned to the maid who had brought them in:

"This young lady will want some tea and bread-and-butter, also."

Irene looked astounded.

The Greek gentleman fixed upon her the steady, sardonic gaze of his dark eyes.

"If you please," he said, with the unctuous sibilance that was the only accent marring the perfection of his English speech.

"I'll see what the manageress says," gasped Irene, and they heard her clattering down the stairs.

The boarders exchanged glances, of which Lydia was perfectly aware, and which did not altogether displease her. She knew that they were all waiting curiously to see the outcome of Irene's mission, and the Greek's reception of its almost certain failure. Miss Nettleship had long ago explained to Lydia that she dared not make any difference in her treatment of the boarders.

"You quite understand how it is, dear, I know. The boarders know very well that your aunt is a friend of mine, and so they're sort of on the look-out for any favouring. And it wouldn't do at all, would it, to have any talk made? It would only be disagreeable for both of us—you know how it is, dear."

Irene reappeared at the door, breathless.

"Miss Nettleship's very sorry, there's no more boiling water," she announced defiantly, and disappeared before the Greek gentleman could do more than look at her, which he did as disagreeably as was possible in the time.

"I am sorry," he remarked gravely to the object of his benevolence.

"It doesn't matter," said Lydia, smiling.

"But it's not right," cried Mr. Bulteel, as though sheer distress were compelling him to break into the conversation contrary to his will, and certainly contrary to his usual habit.

"It's not *right*. One pays for tea, and one ought to have it. She never deducts a meal like tea from the bill, even if one hasn't had it."

His wife tittered shrilly.

"I should think she didn't! It's disgraceful the way that woman charges for the food. No one ever has a second helping."

The room became animated on the instant.

Mr. Bulteel had introduced one of those topics, that, from sheer force of unending discussion in the past, become eagerly acclaimed as suitable for unending discussion in the present.

"I *ask* for a second helping," said old Miss Lillicrap triumphantly. "I *ask* for it. And I get it, too. I had two helpings of the pudding yesterday, and I sent the girl back for some custard. She brought it to me without any custard the second time, but I sent her back for it. It was the disobliging waitress, too, not Irene, and I could see she didn't like it. But she had to go back for the custard, and Miss Nettleship gave it to her. She knew it was for me, and she didn't dare to refuse it."

No one congratulated Miss Lillicrap on her achievement. She was very unpopular, and it was evident that to most of the boarders the recollection sprang to mind vividly of the methods to which she had recourse for the maintenance of her privileges. Indeed, Miss Nettleship had herself told Lydia of her own defeat at the aged but determined hands of Miss Lillicrap, who had once had five cardiac attacks in succession sooner than pay a disputed item on her weekly bill, emerging from each one in order to say, "It's extortionate, and you'll have to take it off. I shan't pay."

When she had said it five times, and showed an iron intention of relapsing into a sixth catalepsy, as a preliminary to saying it again, the manageress had cast up her eyes to heaven, and exclaimed that the charge should be remitted.

Thereafter Miss Lillicrap had the upper hand, and knew it, and Miss Nettleship was wont to say pleadingly to her other boarders:

"You know what it is—Miss Lillicrap is old, and then with her heart and all——"

They resented it, but they also were powerless before those tiny, gnarled hands, that little puckered face nodding and shaking under a lace cap, and that cracked, envenomed old voice.

"I wish there was less custard and more pudding, very often," said Mr. Bulteel, with a sort of gloomy humorousness. "It's always custard."

"Made with custard powder at that," put in his wife.

"Eggs are so expensive," Mrs. Clarence's habitual little whine contributed to the quota.

"Not that we don't pay enough for her to give us real custard made with eggs," she added hastily, lest it should be thought that she was accustomed to economical shifts.

"Hector," said his mother sharply, "have you finished your tea?"

The youth looked resentfully at his parents.

"Go and do your exercises then, my boy," said his father firmly.

"All right, father, all right."

"Now, go at once, Hector," said Mrs. Bulteel, as she always said every evening when her son manifested reluctance with regard to the enforced physical drill, judged by his parents necessary to the well-being of their weedy offspring.

"The boy gets hardly any exercise," his mother discontentedly informed her neighbour, the Greek, who contented himself with casting a disparaging eye over Hector's lanky proportions, as though he thought it entirely immaterial whether these were duly developed or not.

"Wonderful thing, those dumb-bell exercises," remarked Mr. Bulteel, shooting a scraggy wrist out of his coat sleeve, and then withdrawing it again hastily, as an unsuccessful advertisement. "Hurry up, my boy."

The door opened again before Hector had responded in any way to the bracing exhortations of his progenitors.

"Miss Forster back again?" said the Greek gentleman. "We shall have our game of Bridge before dinner, then."

"Don't move, don't move!" cried Miss Forster, breezily putting out a protesting hand very tightly fastened into a white-kid glove, and thereby obliging Mr. Bulteel to rise reluctantly from his arm-chair.

"Oh, what a shame!"

Miss Forster sank into the vacated seat immediately, with a loud sigh of relief.

"Have you had a pleasant afternoon with your friends?" Mrs. Bulteel inquired. She was always inordinately curious about the social engagements of other people, but Miss Forster's garrulousness needed no questionings.

"A topping afternoon!" she declared with youthful slanginess. "Never held such cards, either. What do you think of eight hearts to the Ace, King, Queen?"

The Greek gentleman, to whom she appealed, was non-committal.

"It depends who was holding them," he replied laconically.

"Well, I was, of course. My partner's deal—he'd gone no trumps; they doubled, and of course I redoubled, and we made the little slam. Jolly, eh? though I prefer something with *rather* more play in it, myself."

"Such as last night," grimly suggested the Greek, in unkind allusion to an incident that Miss Forster might reasonably be supposed to prefer forgotten.

"Haven't you forgotten that horrid diamond suit of yours yet?" cried the lady, shaking an admonitory forefinger. "It was certainly a slip, and I can't think how I came to make it."

"You took the lead out of your partner's hand," piped Mrs. Clarence, with a sudden display of knowledge that caused Miss Forster, the recognized Bridge expert of the house until the Greek gentleman's recent arrival, to look at her in astonished resentment.

"I'm not a player, I know," hastily said Mrs. Clarence, perhaps in tardy dread lest she also might be reminded of past fiascos. "Only I always remember that my husband's golden rule used to be, 'Third in hand plays his highest, and second in hand plays his lowest.' I've never forgotten that."

Mrs. Clarence's husband was the only claim to superiority which she could flaunt before the better-dressed, better-housed, better-connected, generally better-off pretensions of Miss Forster and she flaunted him freely.

Perhaps it was on this account that no one paid the slightest attention to the *mot* of the departed card-player.

Mrs. Bulteel picked up the *Daily Sketch*, and said without animation, as without any shred of meaning: "Fancy the Duke of Connaught going to Canada!" and Mr. Bulteel suddenly exclaimed in shocked tones:

"*Hector!* You won't have time to do your exercises before dinner if you don't go at once."

The youth slouched from the room.

"Mr. Hector should hold himself better!" cried Miss Forster, who never hesitated to make a remark on the score of its being a personal one. She flung back her shoulders as she spoke.

"My son is growing very fast," said Mrs. Bulteel stiffly.

Miss Forster laughed.

"Well, I must go and take off my hat."

She slightly lifted the brim of her large hat, as though to render her meaning perfectly clear, and left the room.

Mrs. Bulteel's plain, pinched face was further disfigured by a sneer.

"Poor woman!" she said spitefully. "She really can't afford to criticize other people. She gets stouter every day, I do believe."

"Is she really such a very good Bridge-player?" Mrs. Clarence asked, with a sort of restrained eagerness, as though ashamed of hoping—as she quite obviously did—that the answer would be in the negative.

"She plays a fair game—*for* one of your sex," said the Greek ungallantly.

It was such small observations as this, which he let fall from time to time, that made Lydia feel almost certain that she disliked him, although at other times she was gratified by his half-covert admiration of her.

Presently the Bulteels went in pursuit of Hector and his dumbbells; old Miss Lillicrap tottered off to scream shrilly for hot water from the top of the kitchen stairs, and Mrs. Clarence, glancing at Lydia with a friendly little furtive smirk, sidled out of the room to engage upon one of those mysterious futilities that served to bridge the gaps in the one regular occupation of her life: her attendance at meals.

Lydia and the Greek were left alone together in the drawing-room.

"The days are drawing in very fast," he observed, gazing at the window.

Lydia felt slightly disappointed at the highly impersonal nature of the remark.

"Yes," she said unenthusiastically.

"Do you find the evenings rather long after you get in from your work? You very seldom join us in the drawing-room, I notice, after dinner."

"Sometimes I go and sew in Miss Nettleship's room, and talk to her," said Lydia.

"Sometimes, no doubt. But are there not evenings when you retire to your own apartment very early?"

Lydia reflected that foreigners no doubt held views unshared by the conventional British mind, as to the propriety of expressing a manifest curiosity in the affairs of other people.

"Sometimes I have writing to do," she said shyly.

The admission was not altogether unpremeditated. Lydia knew that the Greek was an insatiable reader, mostly of French novels, and it had occurred to her some time since that he might not unpossibly be of use in advising her. Besides, she owned to herself quite frankly, that his interest in her was not likely to be diminished by the discovery of her literary ambitions.

"I came to London partly so as to be able to write," she told him. "I have wanted to write books ever since I was a child."

"Ever since you were a child!" he repeated with a hint of friendly derision. "That is indeed a long while. And what form does this writing of yours take? No doubt you write poetry—all about love, and springtime, and death?"

Lydia felt herself colouring with annoyance as she replied with decision:

"Dear me, no. I shouldn't think of writing poetry nowadays. I know very well that I can't. But I've written one or two short stories, and I should like one day—to write books."

"Have these stories of yours been published?"

"No, not yet," said Lydia. "I haven't tried to publish them. I don't know if they're the right length, or where to send them, or anything."

"Haven't you ever come across a useful little book called 'The Artist and Author's Handbook?' That would give you all the information you require."

"Would it? I could try and get it," said Lydia doubtfully.

She did not want to spend any extra money. There had proved to be so many unforeseen expenses in London.

"I think I have a copy. Allow me to lend it to you," said the Greek. "It will give you a list of the publishers, and publications, and a great deal of very practical information. You should certainly see it. I will give it to you to-morrow."

"Oh, thank you!"

"In return," said the obliging foreigner, with a slight smile, "may I not be allowed to read one of your tales?"

Lydia, the intuitive, had been mentally anticipating the request. She was eager enough for a verdict upon her work, and only pretended a little modest hesitation.

"I am afraid you wouldn't find them very interesting—but I should like to know if you think there's any hope for me, Mr. ——"

"My name is Margoliouth," said he.

No one else had ever been honoured by the information.

Lydia went upstairs, discreetly taking upon herself to break up the *tête-à-tête*, with increased self-satisfaction.

She was less pleased a few days later when she discovered that everybody in the boarding-house now knew that she wrote stories.

"I'm not a bit surprised," Miss Forster cried loudly and joyously. "I always felt we had a lot in common. Why, I should write myself if I could only find the time."

She traced rapid scribbles in the air with her forefinger.

"It must be a great hobby for you," said pale Mr. Bulteel, looking respectfully at Lydia.

"Perhaps one night you'll read us one of your stories," his wife suggested.

She was not usually gracious to the other women in the house, but Lydia had always listened sympathetically to her account of the agony that she suffered from her teeth, now undergoing extensive structural alterations.

Only little Mrs. Clarence gazed at Lydia with a thoroughly uneasy eye.

"I must say," she said with a note of aggression in her habitual whine, "I do hope you won't put *me* into one of your books, Miss Raymond."

Lydia enjoyed the attention that was bestowed upon her, even while she critically told herself that it lacked discernment.

She did not read her stories out loud to the assembled boarders, as Mrs. Bulteel had suggested, but she submitted several of them to the inspection of Margoliouth.

"They have merit, and originality," he told her. "But your English is not good."

Lydia held out her hand for the manuscripts without replying.

"Aha, you think that a foreigner cannot criticize English," he said acutely, and interpreting her secret thought with perfect correctness. "But I assure you that I am right. Look! you put 'alright' for 'all right' and 'She was very interested' instead of 'she was very much interested.' And again, you have 'under the circumstances' for 'in the circumstances.' All these are common errors. Tell me, what authors do you read?"

Lydia was vague. Like the majority of readers, she chose books almost at random, because the title allured her, or because someone had said that the story was exciting.

The Greek shrugged his shoulders.

"The ideas are there," he said, "but you must learn to express them better."

Lydia felt so much mortified that she could hardly speak. She, the Head of the School at Miss Glover's, the owner of the "mathematical mind" so rarely found in one of her own sex, the responsible and trusted accountant at Elena's, to be told that she could not write

English!

At that moment she disliked Margoliouth with all the cordial dislike accorded to a really candid critic.

Yet it was characteristic of Lydia that, even in the midst of her vexation, she realized that to display it would be to destroy much of the Greek's flattering opinion of her superior intelligence. She drew a long breath, and gazed at him frankly and steadily.

"Thank you very much," she said. "I must try and study the really good writers, and—and I'll remember what you say, and try and write better English. I'm sure you're right."

It was a little set speech, uttered regardless of the indignation still burning within her, and it did not fail of its effect.

"Well done!" cried the Greek softly. "Well done, Miss Raymond! It is very rare to find so much frankness and determination in a lady, if I may say so—I am the more sure that you will eventually succeed."

Lydia thanked him and took away her manuscripts.

She was inwardly just as angry at his criticism as she had been on first hearing it, and just as certain that a foreigner could know nothing about the correctness or otherwise of her English. But she congratulated herself on the presence of mind and strength of will which had enabled her to make so good a show of open-minded generosity. Quite evidently Margoliouth thought the better of her for it, and Lydia would not for the world have forfeited his admiration.

It gave her great *prestige* in the eyes of the other boarders.

Lydia knew that they most of them liked her, Mr. Bulteel because she was young and pretty, his wife, and whining little Mrs. Clarence, because she always listened to them sympathetically, all the while inwardly mindful of Grandpapa's rule—"*Always let the other people talk about themselves.*"

Miss Forster liked her too.

Lydia did not exactly flatter Miss Forster, but she had a tactful way of introducing the topic of Miss Forster's great friends, Sir Rupert and Lady Honoret, and was always ready to hear about the Bridge parties that Miss Forster frequented at their house in Lexham Gardens.

Hector Bulteel, the pallid youth whose days were passed in Gower Street, had at first been too shy even to speak to Lydia, but one day she asked for his advice on a point of accountancy, and thereafter they occasionally discussed the higher mathematics or the distinctions between organic and inorganic chemistry.

Lydia did not really think very highly of Hector's capabilities, but criticized him as shrewdly as she did everyone else with whom she came into contact.

She was always careful, however, to keep her rather caustic judgments to herself, and she knew that both at Madame Elena's and at the boarding-house the reputation that had been hers at school still prevailed: Lydia Raymond never said an unkind thing about anyone.

Even old Miss Lillicrap, who seldom uttered a word that was not either spiteful or complaining, looked at Lydia in a comparatively friendly silence on the evening that the Greek gentleman first took her to the Polytechnic.

Lydia wore a new, pale-pink blouse, and her best dark-brown cloth coat and skirt.

For the first time, she decided that she really *was* pretty.

The conviction lent exhilaration to the evening's entertainment, which on the whole she found rather dull. She was not very much amused by the cinematograph films displayed, and when, towards the end of the evening, Mr. Margoliouth fumbled for her hand in the darkness and held it, Lydia was principally conscious that hers was still sticky from the chocolates that he had given her, and failed to derive any thrill from the experience.

XI

Towards Christmas time, as the evenings became shorter and shorter, Mr. Margoliouth developed great concern at the idea of Lydia's coming back from her work alone.

Might he call for her at Madame Elena's, and escort her home?

Lydia thanked him very much, and said that one of her fellow-workers generally came most of the way with her. But she was not insensible to the flattering vista thus opened.

The girls at Elena's would be, in their own parlance, thrilled if a foreign and interesting-looking male should make his appearance outside the little shop and await there the privilege of accompanying Miss Raymond across the Park.

Gina Ryott boasted a "gentleman friend" who occasionally paid her the same compliment, and Lydia, as well as Marguerite Saxon, had peeped through the closed shutters of the shop window more than once, in order to watch them depart together.

And not only the girls but the community at the boarding-house would be full of interest and excitement.

Already Lydia knew perfectly well that Miss Forster and Mrs. Bulteel exchanged significant glances whilst she and the Greek talked to one another at meals.

In the trivial monotony of the boarding-house existence, she even felt certain that Mr. Margoliouth and his increasingly-marked attentions to herself were the chief subjects of discussion.

She began to enjoy her position very much, and no longer held Mr. Margoliouth at a distance. She was not at all in love with him, but his attentions were very agreeable and certainly, Lydia told herself, he had enough discernment to realize that she was not a person with whom liberties might be taken.

As a fact, his manner towards her was respectful enough except for a certain tendency towards patting her wrist, or attracting her attention by a lingering touch upon her arm or her shoulder.

When they went to a theatre or a cinematograph, he always held her hand, and a curious sense of fair play in return for his hospitality induced Lydia to allow this, and even feebly to return an occasional pressure of her fingers, although she derived no slightest satisfaction from the contact.

The rapid development of her mentality had so far out-distanced other, more human attributes of youth, that she frequently debated within herself whether Mr. Margoliouth was ever likely to try and kiss her. If so, Lydia reflected with cold self-righteousness, she would rebuke him in such fashion that he would respect and admire her more than ever. She was full of instinctive horror at the idea of "making herself cheap," and it had been inculcated into her both by Aunt Beryl and Aunt Evelyn that to do so was to invite disaster of some unspecified but terrible kind.

When her Christmas holiday was approaching—two days and a half which she was to spend at Regency Terrace—Lydia began to mention the Greek occasionally in her weekly letter to Aunt Beryl.

She was not averse from some slight exploitation of her first conquest, and moreover she thought it quite likely that a hint might reach Aunt Beryl any day through Miss Nettleship, and she wisely preferred to secure herself against any charge of secretiveness.

At first Aunt Beryl only wrote back, "Glad you enjoyed yourself at the Polytechnic, dear; mind and not take cold coming out from those hot places this bitter weather." Then later: "This Mr. Margoliouth seems very attractive. Don't let him break your little heart, dear!"

The two notes of exclamation denoted Aunt Beryl's humorous intention, as Lydia well knew. But one day she wrote more seriously.

"I must say it would be a real pleasure to hear you were properly engaged, providing it was to some really nice fellow. Don't be in a hurry to decide though, dear—you're very young."

Lydia herself had hardly contemplated the possibility of an engagement. But now she began to wonder whether or no any such idea held a place in Margoliouth's mind. He had certainly said that he should like to show her his own country, and told her how much she would enjoy a sea voyage and how greatly the new experience of travelling would help her to write.

Meanwhile he continued to take her out two or three times a week, and to give her expensive boxes of chocolates and occasional books.

The girls at Madame Elena's became aware of him, and chaffed Lydia agreeably, and at the boarding-house Miss Forster, always outspoken, one day asked whether she had ordered her wedding-dress yet.

Lydia did not like Miss Forster's blatancy, but her old predilection for finding herself the heroine of her surroundings was stronger than ever, and it gratified her to know that they were all watching her and wondering what would happen to her next.

A less agreeable manifestation of interest was, however, in store for her.

Miss Nettleship sought her out apologetic but conscientious.

"You know how it is, dear, I know—but really I do feel responsible to your auntie, just a wee bit—and I feel I really must say something. They're all talking about it, you know—not saying anything, I don't mean of course, but you know—just talking, like."

The distinction that Miss Nettleship wished to imply between the saying of anything and mere talking about it, was perfectly clear to the resentful and embarrassed Lydia.

True to her instincts, however, she showed none of the resentment and as little as she could of the embarrassment.

"There really isn't anything for anyone to talk about. Mr. Margoliouth is very fond of the theatre, he says, and he hasn't anyone to go with him. It's very kind of him to take me, I think."

"Once here and there," said Miss Nettleship distractedly, "but really, dear, it's getting more than that, and of course it's a bit conspicuous because of his never hardly taking any notice of anyone else. At the Bridge now, when they play in the evenings, he's downright uncivil to poor Mrs. Clarence, and I've heard him very rude to Miss Forster too, though of course she's well able to hold her own. But it makes it all the more marked, his going on the way he does with you."

"I can't help his liking me," said Lydia meekly, but inwardly rather gratified at Miss Nettleship's artless exposition of the distinction that she enjoyed.

"Now don't go thinking I'm blaming you for an instant, dear. I know very well that your auntie's brought you up to be careful, and, besides, I can see for myself you're steady—not one of those girls I call regular *flirts*. But it's your being so young, and there's something else too."

Miss Nettleship hesitated, her pleasant, anxious-looking face much discomposed.

"Really I oughtn't to say anything about it to you, but you do understand how it is, dear—I feel the responsibility of having you here, and your auntie being such a friend of mine and everything, I feel I can't let it go on and not say anything."

"I've written to Aunt Beryl all about Mr. Margoliouth, you

know," said Lydia quickly.

She felt the announcement to be a trump card, and was surprised that Miss Nettleship's harassed expression did not relax.

"I was sure you would, dear—it isn't that. You see the fact is, though I oughtn't to mention it but I know you can be trusted never to pass it on,—the fact is that Mr. Margoliouth, as he calls himself, isn't altogether sound, and I don't know that I shan't have to ask him to leave."

"Why?" cried Lydia, astonished.

But Miss Nettleship had her own methods of imparting information, and was not to be hustled out of them.

"Of course you know how it is in a place like this—one has to be very particular, and I've always asked for references and everything, and there's never been any trouble except just once, right at the start. That was with foreigners, too, a pair of Germans, and called themselves brother and sister. However, that's nothing to do with you, dear, and I had to send them packing very quickly—in fact, the minute I had any doubts at all. It's the ruin of a place like this ever to let it get a name, as you can imagine, and the fright I got then made me more particular than ever. This fellow Margoliouth gave me a City reference, and another a clergyman somewhere up in Yorkshire, and paid his first week in advance. And since then it's just been one put off after another."

"But how—what do you mean, Miss Nettleship?"

"He's not paying his way," said the manageress, fixing her brown eyes compassionately upon Lydia's face.

"He asked me to let him have his account monthly, as it was more convenient, and I gave in, although it's not my rule, and I wouldn't have that old Miss Lillicrap—you know what she is, dear, and how one can't go against her—I wouldn't have her hear about it for the world. Well, it was seven weeks before he paid me the first month, and I had to ask him for it again and again. He said there was some difficulty about getting his money from Greece paid into the Bank here. However, he paid in the end, but since then it's been nothing but putting off and putting off—would I let it stand over for a week because it wasn't convenient, and so on and so on. I told him he'd have to get his meals out if it went on, and then he gave me something on account—but not a third of what he owes me, dear. I really don't know what to do about it. He's so plausible, I half believe it's all right when he's talking to me, but I can't afford to go on like this. He'll have to go if he hasn't paid in full at the end of this week. And how I'm to get the money back if he doesn't pay up I really don't know, for a prosecution would be a fearful business for me, and lose me every boarder in the place."

"Oh, it would be dreadful!" cried Lydia, sincerely shocked. "But he *must* pay. I thought of him as quite rich."

"So you might, from the way he goes on. And the bills that are always coming for him, too!" said Miss Nettleship.

"I can't help seeing them, you know, when I clear the box in the mornings. However, he says there's money coming to him from Greece, and it's only got to be put into his Bank over here, and he can promise me a cheque on Saturday at latest. So I'm not saying any more till then, but *after* that my mind's made up. But you'll understand, dear, why I felt I had to speak to you about it first."

Lydia felt that she understood only too well, and she went to business next morning in so thoughtful a mood that Rosie Graham, whose observation nothing escaped, made sharp inquiry of her as they snatched a ten minutes' tea-interval in the afternoon: "What's up that you're going about with a face as long as a fiddle?"

In the midst of her perfectly real preoccupation, it was not in Lydia to fail to perceive her opportunity for at last arousing a tardy interest in Miss Graham.

"I'm worried," she said frankly.

"Worry won't mend matters," quoted Rosie tritely, but Lydia reaped the advantage of her invariable abstention from the airing of daily minor grievances such as the other girls brought to their work, in the instant acceptance of her statement shown by the astute little Cockney.

"Come round to my place for a yarn this evening," she suggested. "My pal's out and I can find some food, I daresay, though it won't be seven courses and a powdered footman behind the chair, like that place of yours."

Lydia accepted, and felt flattered. No one else had ever been asked to Rosie's place.

They took a Sloane Street omnibus at six o'clock, and got out at Sloane Square, where Lydia made use of a public telephone to inform Miss Nettleship that she would not be in to supper, and then Rosie led her through a very large square, a mews, and into a little street called Walton Street. They crossed it, and entered Ovington Street.

"Number ninety-one A," said Miss Graham, producing a latchkey.

She took Lydia to the top of the house, and Lydia was astounded at the lightness and airiness of the fair-sized room, with a much smaller one opening out of it, evidently in use as a dressing-room.

"Not so dusty, is it?" Rosie said complacently. "This sofa turns into a bed, and there's another proper bed in the other room. The whole thing—unfurnished—costs us twenty-two and six a week, and includes everything except the use of the gas. There's a penny-in-the-slot machine for that. We do most of our cooking on the gas-ring, but the landlady's very decent about sometimes letting us use the kitchen fire."

She gave Lydia a supper of sausage-rolls, bread-and-butter, co-coa and a variety of sweet cakes and biscuits, and all the time talked more agreeably and less caustically than Lydia had ever heard her talk before.

When the little meal was over and the table pushed out of the way, Rosie made Lydia draw her chair close to the tiny oil-stove.

"There's a gas-fire," she said frankly, "but we don't use it unless the weather's simply perishing. It's rather an expensive luxury. Sure you're all right like that?"

"Yes, thank you. What a lot of heat this thing gives out!"

"Doesn't it? Well, now," said Miss Graham abruptly, "spit it out. What's all the trouble? Is it anything to do with that foreign freak who stands about waiting for you outside Elena's of an evening sometimes?"

Lydia was too well inured to the shop-girl vocabulary to resent this description of her admirer.

She decided that she would allow herself the luxury of contra-vening Grandpapa's rule, and for once talk about herself, justified in doing so by her conviction that it was the only short cut to the rous-ing in Miss Rosie Graham of that interest which Lydia still desired the more keenly from the very ease with which she could command it in others.

She told her story, but omitted all mention of Miss Nettleship's confidences.

"My aunt, who brought me up, knows a little about it—I wrote and told her he was taking me out sometimes—and she said in a let-ter I had from her the other day that it would be so nice if I got en-gaged. Somehow, you know, I hadn't really thought of that before. But I've been rather worried since, wondering whether perhaps he means to ask me. If so, I suppose I oughtn't to let him go about with me quite so much unless I make up my mind to say 'yes.'"

Lydia was aware that she had stated her problem one-sidedly, for her real preoccupation was whether or no Margoliouth was going to pay her the compliment of a proposal. But the temptation to represent herself as merely undecided if she should become engaged to him or not, was irresistible.

She thought that Rosie looked at her rather curiously as she finished speaking.

"Of course, if you're always about with him and let him give you presents and all the rest of it, the poor Johnnie's bound to think you mean business," she said slowly. "But you'd better be careful, kid. Are you so sure that he wants to marry you?"

Lydia felt herself colouring hotly, sufficiently understanding the older girl's implication to resent it.

"I should think Mr. Margoliouth is too much of a man of the world not to see for himself the sort of girl *I* am," she said haughtily.

"He can see for himself that you're only a silly kid, if that's what you mean," retorted the outspoken Rosie Graham. "Tell me, where does this Margoliouth, or whatever he calls himself, come from? He's as black as my hat, anyway."

Lydia began to wish that she had never embarked upon the path of confidences at all.

"He is Greek," she said very stiffly.

"That might mean anything," retorted Miss Graham sweepingly. "I tell you frankly that's what I don't like about the business—his being such a rum colour. I don't trust black fellows."

"You talk as though he were a nigger!" said Lydia, furious.

"I know what I'm talking about. I knew a girl once who took up with a fellow like that. He wasn't a bit darker than your Margoliouth, and he talked awfully good English, and she got herself engaged to him. He said he was a prince, and frightfully rich, and he gave her all sorts of presents, and when he had to go back to his own country he sent her the money for her passage so she could come out next year and get married to him. Well, she got everything ready—heaps of clothes and things—and was always talking of how she was going to be a princess, and he'd promised to meet her at a place called Port Said with his own carriage and horses and all the rest of it. Some of us thought she was taking a bit of a risk, but she didn't care a scrap, and was just wild to get out there. Well, off she went—and we didn't hear anything more about her, or get any of the letters and photographs and things she'd promised to send. And then three months later, I met her in the City, where I was matching silks for old Peroxide, and she'd sneaked back to her old firm and got them to take her back as typist again."

"But what had happened?"

"She didn't tell me, and I didn't ask her. But she told another girl, and I heard about it afterwards. She'd gone off on the ship all right, with all her fine new luggage and the rest of it, and she'd told all the people on board who she was going out to marry, and most of them said what a fool she was, and it would be an awful life for an English girl, and she'd never be allowed to come home again. But there was one man on board—a parson—who simply wouldn't let her alone about it, and said she didn't know what she was doing, and at last he got her to promise that she wouldn't actually marry this chap until he'd made inquiries about him. And he did the minute they arrived—although the fellow was there just as he'd said, with a great carriage and two horses, to take her away. I don't exactly know what happened, but this clergyman fellow went straight off to some British Consul or someone, and they found out all about the man straight away. He *was* a sort of prince all right, and quite as rich as he'd said—though he didn't live in a palace, but some place right away from everywhere—but he wasn't a Christian—and *he'd got two native wives already.*"

"Oh!" Lydia gasped involuntarily at the climax of the narrative, which came upon her inexperience as a complete shock.

"So that was the end of *that*, as you can imagine," said Miss Graham. "The clergyman was awfully good to her, and paid her passage home again out of his own pocket, because she hadn't got a sixpence. Poor kid, she was fearfully cut up, though as a matter of fact she ought to have been off her head with thankfulness that she got stopped in time. I don't suppose she'd ever have got away again, once he'd taken her off in his carriage and pair."

"It must have been awful for her, going back to her old job, after leaving it to get married like that," said Lydia. She thought with horror of the humiliation that it would mean for the victim to return, in such circumstances, to those who had doubtless heard her triumphant boasts of emancipation on leaving.

"D'you think that would be the worst of it?" queried Miss Graham sharply.

Lydia, failing to see the drift of the question, answered unhesitatingly:

"Yes, I think it would. It's the part *I* should have minded most."

A guilty remembrance flashed across her mind of yet another axiom of Grandpapa's—"Don't refer everything back to yourself."

She wished that she had remembered it earlier, when Rosie looked at her strangely, and then said:

"I believe you *would* mind that most—what other people would say and think about you, I mean. What an inhuman kid you are!"

Lydia felt almost more bewildered than offended.

"Isn't there anybody you care for beside yourself?" said Rosie Graham slowly. "I've been watching you ever since you came to us. Of course you're very clever, and a cut above the rest of us—I know all that—and you're awfully sweet and nice to everybody, and never say cattish things about anyone—but what's it all *for*? You don't care a damn for anybody that I can see. And then you talk about this chap who's going with you—this Margoliouth—and whether he wants you to be engaged or not. And I don't believe you've once thought whether you could care for him, or he for you. Why, this girl I was telling you about was crazy about her fellow. *That* was what broke her up—not the having made a fool of herself, and wondering if the others at her old shop weren't laughing at her. But that's simply beyond you, isn't it? I don't believe you know what caring for anybody means."

The two girls looked at one another in silence.

Rosie's accusation not only came as a shock to Lydia, but it carried with it an inward conviction that was disconcerting in the extreme.

Lydia, no coward, faced the unpalatable truth, and instinctively and instantly accepted it as such.

She wondered, with the curious analytical detachment characteristic of the self-centred, that she had never seen it for herself. It vexed her that it should have been left to little Rosie Graham's penetration to enlighten her.

She rallied her forces. Rosie should at least see in her the saving grace of a courageous candour.

"Perhaps that's true," she said slowly. "I've been first with one set of people, and then with another, since I was a small child, and perhaps I've got into a calculating way of just trying to please them, so that they should be nice to me. I don't know that I'm really particularly fond of any of them...."

She passed in mental review as she spoke those with whom her short life had been most nearly connected.

Her parents.

She could hardly remember her father, and she had certainly never loved her mother, weak where Lydia, at twelve years old, was already hard, irrationally impulsive where Lydia was calculating, sentimental where Lydia was contemptuous. Looking back, she realized that her mother had done her best to make Lydia as feebly emotional as she was herself, and that Lydia's own clear-sightedness had not only saved her, but had also forced upon her a very thorough reaction.

Grandpapa—Aunt Beryl—Uncle George—she thought of them all. Certainly she was fond of them in a way, and Grandpapa she most sincerely admired and respected, more than anyone she knew.

She was grateful to Aunt Beryl and Uncle George, and anxious to do them credit, but her interest in their welfare was not excessive. If she heard of their deaths that evening, Lydia knew very well that her chief pang would be remorse for a complete absence of acute sorrow.

There was Nathalie Palmer.

At school, Nathalie had adored her. She still wrote her long, intimate letters full of personal details which Lydia could not help thinking rather trivial and unnecessary.

But because one criticized, that did not preclude a certain degree of affection. Lydia was certainly fond of Nathalie.

She did not for an instant, however, pretend either to herself or to Rosie Graham, that the latter's words were unjustified by fact.

"I'm certainly not at all in love with Mr. Margoliouth now," she said, "but there's no reason why I shouldn't be later on, I suppose. And because it's more or less true that I've never cared a very great deal for anybody so far, it doesn't follow that I never shall. I'm not twenty yet."

"I suppose there's hope for you," said Rosie Graham grudgingly. "But I'm very sorry for you when you once *do* begin to care for somebody—I don't mind who it may be."

Lydia was conscious of feeling rather flattered by the interpretation she put upon the words.

"I suppose that all one's eggs in one basket is always a risk," she said, not without complacency.

Rosie gave a short, staccato laugh, and again shot one of her disconcerting glances at her visitor.

"What *I* mean is that you'll do it so jolly badly. You've never cared for anybody but yourself, and you won't even know how to begin."

"Then you had better be sorry for the person I care for," said Lydia drily.

She was in reality very angry, and she rose to go for fear of betraying it.

"I daresay it's rather beastly of me to have said that, when I've asked you here to spend the evening," said Rosie with a certain compunction in her voice.

"I'm very glad you said what you thought," Lydia returned calmly. "Good night, and thanks for having me."

"Good night. And I say—*don't* do anything in a hurry about that coloured friend of yours."

Lydia walked downstairs and out of the front door without deigning any reply to this last, urgent piece of advice.

As she sat in the jolting, nearly empty omnibus that was to take her as far as Southampton Row, she reviewed Rosie Graham's speeches of the evening.

It was quite true, Lydia supposed, that she did not really care for anybody but herself. She was too clear-sighted to pretend that this distressed her. On the contrary, she realized the immense simplification of a life into which no seriously conflicting claims could enter.

After all it had taken the almost uncanny acumen of a Rosie Graham to discover the fundamental egotism that underlay all Lydia's careful courtesy and studied kindness of word and deed.

She was annoyed that Rosie should have so poor an opinion of her, but Rosie was only one person; and though in Lydia's present surroundings she held rank of high importance, the importance was merely relative.

The day would come when Rosie Graham, and what Rosie Graham thought, whether true or otherwise, would matter not at all to Lydia Raymond.

XII

NEVERTHELESS, Rosie Graham's anecdote of the girl who had gone to Port Said, and her vehement advice to have nothing to do with the Greek, continued to haunt Lydia's mind.

Neither had she forgotten Miss Nettleship's warning, and the sense that the manageress was watching her with melancholy anxiety caused her to surmise that Mr. Margoliouth had not yet made good his assurance of payment.

She refused an invitation to go to the play with him, but was too anxious that the boarders should continue to look upon her as the heroine of an exciting love-affair to discourage him altogether, although she had really made up her mind that she should not care to be engaged to Margoliouth.

If the first man who had made her acquaintance since she left school showed so much tendency to make love to her, Lydia shrewdly told herself, there would certainly be others. She could well afford to wait, in the certainty of eventually finding a man who would possess such attractions and advantages as the Greek could not boast.

Meanwhile, Margoliouth made life interesting, and Lydia a subject of universal observation and discussion.

She was feeling agreeably conscious of this on the Saturday following her conversation with the manageress, as she came into the boarding-house in time for the midday meal.

Miss Nettleship was hovering at the foot of the stairs and failed to return Lydia's smile.

"He'll have to go," she said without preliminary. "I got his cheque, and the Bank has returned it. You see how it is, dear—a terrible business. I don't know whether I shan't have to call the police in even now before I get my money. He's leaving on Monday, and if I've not had the cash down from him, I don't know what'll happen, I'm sure."

"Oh, Miss Nettleship, how dreadful! I *am* sorry for you," said Lydia, giving expression to the surface emotion of her mind only, from habit and instinct alike.

"Don't you have anything more to do with him, dear," said Miss Nettleship distractedly. "That Agnes is letting something burn downstairs. I can smell it as plain as anything. I'll have to go. Poor old Agnes! she means well but you quite understand how it is——"

The manageress hastened down the stairs to the basement.

Lydia could not help glancing at her neighbour in the dining-room with a good deal of anxiety. He seemed quite imperturbable, and said nothing about his departure.

Lydia, whose opinion of Miss Nettleship's mentality was not an exalted one, began to think that Mr. Margoliouth knew quite well that he could pay his bills before Monday, and had no intention of going away at all.

Otherwise, why was he not more uneasy? Far from uneasy, Margoliouth seemed to be livelier than usual, paid Lydia one or two small compliments with his usual half-condescending, half-sardonic expression, and asked her if she would come out to tea with him that afternoon.

Miss Nettleship was on one of her periodical excursions to the kitchen, and Miss Forster, Mrs. Clarence, and Mrs. Bulteel were listening with all their ears, and with as detached an expression as each could contrive to assume.

"Thank you very much, I should like to," said Lydia demurely.

They went to a newly-opened corner shop in Piccadilly, where a small orchestra was playing, and little shaded pink lights stood upon all the tables. The contrast with the foggy December dusk outside struck pleasantly upon Lydia's imagination, and she enjoyed herself, and was talkative and animated.

Margoliouth stared at her with his unwinking black gaze, and when they had finished tea he left his chair, and came to sit beside her on the low plush sofa, that had its back to the wall.

"A girl like you shouldn't go about London alone," he suddenly remarked, with a sort of unctuousness. "At least, not until she knows something about life."

"Oh, I can take care of myself," said Lydia hastily.

"But you don't know the dangers that a young girl of your attraction is exposed to," he persisted. "You don't know what sort of brutes men can be, do you?"

"No girl need ever be annoyed—unless she *wants* to be," quoted Lydia primly from Aunt Beryl's wisdom.

"You think so, do you? Now, I wonder if you'll still say that in three years' time. Do you know that you are the sort of woman to make either a very good saint or a very good sinner?"

The world-old lure was too potent for Lydia's youth and her vanity.

"Am I?" she said eagerly. "Sometimes I've thought that, too."

The Greek put his hand upon her, slipping his arm through hers in his favourite manner.

"Tell me about your little self, won't you?" he said ingratiatingly. *"Always let the other people talk about themselves."*

Oh, inconvenient and ill-timed recollection of Grandpapa's high, decisive old voice! So vividly was it forced upon the ear of Lydia's unwilling memory that she could almost have believed herself at Regency Terrace once more. The illusion checked her eager, irrepressible grasp at the opportunity held out by the foreigner. The game was spoilt.

"There's nothing to tell," she said abruptly, suddenly grown weary.

Grandpapa had said that long stories about oneself always bored other people, whether or no they politely affected an appearance of interest.

No doubt it was true.

Lydia knew that she herself was not apt to take any very real interest, for instance, in Nathalie Palmer's long letters about her home, and the parish, and the new experiment of keeping hens at the vicarage, nor in the many stories, all of them personal, told by the girls at Elena's, nor even in the monotonous recital of Miss Nettleship's difficulties with her servants.

Why should the Greek be interested in hearing Lydia's opinion of Lydia?

She cynically determined that it would not be worth while to put him to the test.

"Let's go home," she said.

Margoliouth raised his eyebrows.

"I suppose that all women are capricious."

His use of the word "women," as applied to her nineteen-year-old self, always insensibly flattered Lydia.

She let him take her back to the Bloomsbury boarding-house in a hansom, and remained passive, although unresponsive, when he put his arm round her, and pressed her against him in the narrow confinement of the cab.

"Dear little girl!" sighed Margoliouth sentimentally, as he reluctantly released her from his clasp when the cab stopped.

Lydia ran up the steps, agreeably surprised at the instant opening of the door, and anxious to exchange the raw and foggy atmosphere outside for the comparative warmth and light of the hall.

The dining-room door also stood open, and as Lydia came in Miss Forster rushed out upon her.

"I've been waiting for you!" she cried effusively. "Come in here, my dear, won't you?"

"Into the dining-room?" said Lydia, amazed. "Why, there's no fire there! I'm going upstairs."

"No, no," said Miss Forster still more urgently, and laying a tightly-gloved white-kid hand on Lydia's arm. "There's someone up there."

She pointed mysteriously to the ceiling.

Lydia looked up, bewildered, but only saw Miss Nettleship, the gas-light shining full on her pale, troubled face, hastening down the stairs. She passed Lydia and Miss Forster unperceiving, and went straight up to the Greek, who had just closed the street door behind him.

"Mr. Margoliouth!" she said, in her usual breathless fashion. "You see how it is—it's quite all right, I'm sure ... but your wife has come. She's in the drawing-room."

Margoliouth uttered a stifled exclamation, and then went upstairs without another word.

Miss Forster almost dragged Lydia into the dining-room.

"There! Of course you didn't know he was married, did you? Neither did any of us, and I must say I think he's behaved abominably."

"But who is she? When did she come?" asked Lydia, still wholly bewildered at the suddenness of the revelation.

"Sit down, and I'll tell you all about it."

Miss Forster settled her ample person in a chair, with a general expression of undeniable satisfaction.

"Just about half an hour after you'd left the house, I was just wondering if I should find dear Lady Honoret at home if I ran round—you know my great friends, Sir Rupert and Lady Honoret. I'm sure I've often mentioned them; they're quite well-known people—but I thought, of course, there wouldn't be a chance of finding them disengaged—she's always *somewhere*—so Mrs. Bulteel and I were settling down to a nice, cosy time over the fire. Irene had actually made up quite a good fire, for once. And then the door opened"—Miss Forster flung open an invisible portal with characteristic energy—"and in comes Miss Nettleship—and I remember thinking to myself at the time, in a sort of flash, you know: Miss Nettleship looks *pale*—a sort of startled look—it just flashed through my mind. And this woman was just behind her."

"What is she like?"

Lydia was conscious of disappointment and humiliation, but she was principally aware of extreme curiosity.

"Just what you'd expect," said Miss Forster, with a decisiveness that somehow mitigated the extremely cryptic nature of the description. "The moment I saw her and realized who she was—and I'm bound to say Miss Nettleship spoke her name *at once*—that moment I said to myself that she was just what I should have expected her to be."

Lydia, less eager for details of Miss Forster's remarkable prescience than for further information, still looked at her inquiringly.

"Dark, you know," said Miss Forster. "Very dark—and stout."

She described a circle of immense and improbable width. "Older than he is, I should say—without a doubt. And wearing a white veil, and one of those foreign-looking black hats tilted right over her eyes—you know the sort of thing. And boots—buttoned boots. With a check costume—exactly like a foreigner."

"I suppose she *is* a foreigner."

"I spoke in French at once," said Miss Forster. "It was most awkward, of course—and I could see that Mrs. Bulteel was completely taken aback. Not much *savoir faire* there, between ourselves, is there? But, of course, as a woman of the world, I spoke up at once, the moment Miss Nettleship performed the introduction. '*Comment vous trouvez-vous, M'dahme?*' I said. Of course, not shaking hands—simply bowing."

"What did she say?" Lydia asked breathlessly, as Miss Forster straightened herself with a little gasp, after a stiff but profound inclination of her person from the waist downwards.

"She answered in English. She has an accent, of course—doesn't speak nearly as well as he does. Something about us knowing her husband. 'Do you mean Mr. Margoliouth?' I said. Naughty of me, though, wasn't it?"

"Yes, very," said Lydia hastily. "But what did she say?"

"Took it quite seriously," crowed Miss Forster, suddenly convulsed. "Really, some people have *no* sense of the ludicrous. I said it for a bit of mischief, you know. 'Do you mean Mr. Margoliouth?' I said—and she answered me quite solemnly, 'Yes, of course.'"

Then it really was Margoliouth's wife. Lydia began to realize the fact that until now had carried no sort of conviction to her mind.

Margoliouth, a married man, had been making a fool of her before all these people. Such was the aspect of her case that flashed across her with sudden, furious indignation.

She perceived that Miss Forster was looking at her with curiosity.

"I didn't know that he was married at all," said Lydia calmly.

"No one could have guessed it for a moment, and he never gave us a hint," said Miss Forster indignantly. "You won't mind me saying, dear, that I wanted to get you in here and tell you quietly before you went up and found her there, sitting on the sofa as calm as you please."

"Thank you," said Lydia. "But really, you know, it doesn't matter to me if Mr. Margoliouth *is* married. Only I think he ought to have told Miss Nettleship, and—and all of us."

"The cad!" cried Miss Forster energetically, and striking the rather tight lap of her silk dress with a violence that threatened to split the white-kid glove. "What we women have to put up with, I always say! Only a man could behave like that, and what can we do to defend ourselves? Nothing at all. I was telling Sir Rupert Honoret the other day—those friends of mine who live in Lexham Gardens, you know—I was telling him what I thought of the whole sex. Oh, I've the courage of my opinions, I know. Men are brutes—there's no doubt about it."

"I suppose he didn't expect her here?" said Lydia dreamily, still referring to the Margoliouth *ménage*.

Miss Forster understood.

"Not he! You saw what a fool he looked when the manageress told him she was here. She's come to fetch him away, that's what it is. She as good as said so. But they'll be here till Monday morning, I'm afraid—the pair of them. Ugh!——" Miss Forster gave a most realistic shudder. "I don't know how I shall sit at table with them. Miss Nettleship has no business to take in people of that sort—she ought to have made inquiries about the man in the first place, and I shall tell her so."

"Oh, no," said Lydia gently. "Please don't. She'll be so upset at the whole thing already."

"Very generous!" Miss Forster declared, her hand pressed heavily on Lydia's shoulder. "Of course, it's you one can't help thinking of—a young girl like you. Oh, the cad! If I were a man, I'd horsewhip a fellow like that."

She indulged in a vigorous illustrative pantomime.

"I shall be all right," Lydia said quickly—insensibly adopting the most dignified attitude at her command.

She moved to the door.

"Have some supper sent up to your room, do," urged Miss Forster. "I'm sure Irene would get a tray ready, and I'll bring it up to you myself. Then you won't have to come down to the dining-room."

"Thank you very much, but I'd rather come down."

Lydia was speaking literal truth, as, with her usual clear-sightedness, she soon began to realize.

Not only was her curiosity undeniably strong, both to behold the recent arrival, and to observe Margoliouth's behaviour in these new and undoubtedly disconcerting circumstances—but it was slowly borne in upon her that she could not afford to relinquish the opportunity of standing in the lime-light with the attention of her entire audience undeviatingly fixed upon herself.

Her humiliation could be turned into a triumph.

Lydia set her teeth.

She had been very angry with Margoliouth, and was so still—less because he had deceived her than because the discovery of his deceit must destroy all her prestige as the youthful recipient of exclusive attentions. But after all, she could still be the heroine of this boarding-house drama.

Lydia reflected grimly that there were more ways than one of being a heroine.

She looked at herself in the glass. Anger and excitement had given her a colour, and she did not feel at all inclined to cry. She was, in fact, perfectly aware that she was really not in the least unhappy. But the people downstairs would think that she was proudly concealing a broken heart.

Lydia dressed her thick mass of hair very carefully, thrust the high, carved comb into one side of the great black twist at just the right angle, and put on a blouse of soft, dark-red silk that suited her particularly well.

There was a knock at her door.

Lydia went to open it, and saw Miss Nettleship on the threshold.

"Oh, my dear, I am so sorry, and if you want a tray upstairs for this once, it'll be quite all right, and I'll give the girl the order myself. You aren't thinking of coming down to-night, are you?"

"Yes, I am," said Lydia steadily. "It's very kind of you, but I'd rather come down just as usual."

"It's as you like, of course," said the manageress in unhappy accents. "Miss Forster came to me about you—you know what she is. But I'm so vexed you should have heard all in a minute like, only you understand how it was, dear, don't you? And his wife has paid up the bills, all in cash, and wants to stay over Sunday."

"There's the bell," said Lydia.

"Then I must go, dear—you know how it is. That old Miss Lill-icrap is such a terror with the vegetables. I do feel so vexed about it all—and your auntie will be upset, won't she? Are you ready, dear?"

Lydia saw that the kind woman was waiting to accompany her downstairs to the dining-room, but she had every intention of making her entrance unescorted.

"I'm not quite ready," she said coolly. "Please don't wait—I know you want to be downstairs."

The manageress looked bewildered, and as though she felt herself to have been rebuffed, but she spoke in her usual rather incoherently good-natured fashion as she hastened down the stairs.

"Just whatever you like, and it'll be quite all right. I quite understand. I wish I could wait, dear, but really I daren't...."

Lydia was very glad that Miss Nettleship dared not wait.

She herself remained upstairs for another full five minutes, although her remaining preparations were easily completed in one.

At the end of the five minutes she felt sure that all the boarders must be assembled. Hardly anyone was ever late for a meal, since meals for most of the women, at any rate, contributed the principal variety in the day's occupation.

Nevertheless, Lydia went downstairs very slowly, until the sound of clattering plates and dishes, broken by occasional outbreaks of conversation, told her that dinner was in progress.

Then she quickly opened the dining-room door.

They were all there, and they all looked up as she came in.

Her accustomed seat at the far end of the table, next to the Greek, was empty, but on Margoliouth's other side sat a strange woman, whom Lydia was at no pains to identify, even had Miss Forster's description not at once returned to her mind. "Very dark—and stout—and dressed like a foreigner."

Mrs. Margoliouth was all that.

Lydia saw the room and everyone in it, in a flash, as she closed the door behind her.

Miss Lillicrap, clutching her knife and fork, almost as though she were afraid that her food might be snatched from her plate while she peered across the room with eager, malevolent curiosity—Miss Nettleship, suddenly silent in the midst of some babbled triviality, and evidently undecided whether to get up or to remain seated—Mrs. Bulteel, her sharp gaze fixed upon Lydia and her pinched mouth half open—Miss Forster, also staring undisguisedly—Mrs.

Clarence, with her foolish, red-rimmed eyes almost starting from her head—the youth, Hector Bulteel, his mouth still half-full and a tumbler arrested in mid-career in his hand—his father's sallow face turned towards the door, wrinkled with an evident discomfiture.

Mrs. Margoliouth herself had raised a pair of black, hostile-looking eyes, set in a heavy, pasty face, to fix them upon Lydia.

Irene had stopped her shuffling progress round the table, and turned her head over her shoulder.

Only Margoliouth remained with his head bent over his plate, apparently absorbed in the food that he was sedulously cutting up into small pieces.

In the momentary silence Lydia advanced. Her heart was beating very quickly, but she was conscious of distinct exhilaration, and she remembered to tilt her chin a little upward and to walk slowly.

There was the sudden scraping of a chair, and pale, ugly Mr. Bulteel had sprung forward, and come down the room to meet her.

The unexpected little act of chivalry, which obviously came as a surprise to himself as to everybody else, nearly startled Lydia out of her predetermined composure.

She looked up at him and smiled rather tremulously, and he pulled out her chair for her, and waited until she was seated before returning to his own place again.

The meal went on, and the atmosphere was electric. Contrary to her custom, Miss Nettleship made no attempt at introducing the new-comer, and Margoliouth did not seek to rectify the omission.

He ate silently, his eyes on his plate. Twice Lydia addressed small, commonplace remarks to him, each time in the midst of a silence, wherein her voice sounded very clear and steady. He answered politely but briefly, and the other women at the table exchanged glances, and one or two of them looked admiringly at Lydia.

It was this consciousness that kept her outwardly composed, for she found the position far more of an ordeal than she had expected it to be. She was even aware that, under the table, a certain nervous trembling that she could not repress was causing her knees to knock together.

She felt very glad when the meal was over and old Miss Lillicrap—who always gave the signal for dispersal—had pushed her chair back, and said venomously:

"Well, I can't say, 'Thank you for my good dinner.' The fowl was tough, and I didn't get my fair share of sauce with the pudding."

"Are we having a rubber to-night?" Miss Forster inquired loudly of no one in particular, with the evident intention of silencing Miss Lillicrap.

Lydia saw Mrs. Bulteel frown and shake her head, as though in warning.

Margoliouth, however, had at last looked up.

"I'm not playing to-night," he said sullenly.

"Doesn't your wife play Bridge?" Miss Forster inquired rather maliciously.

"No."

"You're tired with your journey perhaps," piped Mrs. Clarence, looking inquisitively at the stranger.

Mrs. Margoliouth stared back at her with lack-lustre and rather contemptuous-looking black eyes.

"What journey?" she said in a thick voice. "I've only come up from Clapham, where we go back on Monday. Our house is at Clapham. The children are there."

"The children?" repeated Mrs. Clarence foolishly.

"We have five children," said Mrs. Margoliouth impassively, but she cast a fierce glance at her husband as she spoke.

Miss Forster suddenly thrust herself forward, and demonstratively put her arm round Lydia's waist.

"I suppose you're going upstairs to your scribbling, as usual, you naughty girl?" she inquired affectionately.

"I ought to," Lydia said, smiling faintly. "It isn't cold in my room now that I've got a little oil-stove. I got the idea from a girl I went to supper with the other night, who lives in rooms."

"How splendid!" said Miss Forster, with loud conviction, her tone and manner leaving no room for doubt that she was paying a tribute to something other than the inspiration of the oil-stove.

Lydia smiled again, and went upstairs.

The other boarders were going upstairs too, and as Lydia turned the corner of the higher flights that led to her own room, she could hear them on the landing below.

"I do think that girl's behaving most splendidly!"

Miss Forster's emphatic superlatives were unmistakable.

"She looks like a sort of queen to-night," said an awed voice, that Lydia recognized with surprise as belonging to the usually inarticulate Hector Bulteel.

She had not missed her effect, then.

Lydia did not write that evening. She went to bed almost at once, glad of the darkness, and feeling strangely tired. After she was in bed she even found, to her own surprise, that she was shedding tears that she could not altogether check at will.

Then, after all, she *minded*?

Lydia could not analyze her own emotion, and as the strain of the day relaxed, she quietly cried herself to sleep like a child.

But the eventual analysis of the whole episode, made by Lydia with characteristic detachment, brought home to her various certainties.

Margoliouth's defection had hurt her vanity slightly—her heart not at all.

She could calmly look back upon her brief relations with him as experience, and therefore to be valued.

But perhaps the conviction that penetrated her mind most strongly, was that one which she faced with her most unflinching cynicism, although it would have vexed her to put it into words for any other human being. No grief or bereavement that her youth was yet able to conceive of could hurt her sufficiently to discount the lasting and fundamental satisfaction of the *beau rôle* that it would bestow upon her in the view of the onlookers.

XIII

"Broken heart? Nonsense. People with broken hearts don't eat chestnut-pudding like that," quoth Grandpapa.

Lydia would have preferred to make her own explanations at Regency Terrace, but Miss Nettleship had already written a long letter to Aunt Beryl, as Lydia discovered when she reached home on Christmas Eve.

Aunt Beryl took the affair very seriously, and made Lydia feel slightly ridiculous.

"Trifling like that with a young girl, and him a married man the whole of the time!" said Aunt Beryl indignantly.

"It's all *right*, auntie," Lydia made rather impatient answer. "I didn't take it seriously, you know."

"How did he know you weren't going to? Many a girl has had her heart broken for less."

It was then that Grandpapa uttered his unkind allusion to Lydia's undoubted appreciation of her favourite chestnut-pudding, made in honour of her arrival by Aunt Beryl herself.

Lydia knew very well that Grandpapa would have been still more disagreeable if she had pretended a complete loss of appetite, and she felt rather indignant that this very absence of affectation should thus come in for criticism.

Although she had only been away four months, the house seemed smaller, and the conversation of Aunt Beryl and Uncle George more restricted. She was not disappointed when her aunt told her that their Christmas dinner was to be eaten at midday, and that there would be guests.

"Who do you think is here, actually staying at the 'Osborne'?" Miss Raymond inquired.

Lydia was unable to guess.

"Your Aunt Evelyn, with Olive. They've been worried about Olive for quite a time now—she can't throw off a cold she caught in the autumn, and, of course, there *have* been lungs in the Senthoven family, so they're a bit uneasy. Aunt Evelyn brought her down here for a change, and Bob's coming down for Christmas Day. They keep him very busy at the office now. Don't you ever run across him in town, Lydia?"

"No, never," said Lydia, with great decision.

She had no wish to meet Bob Senthoven in London, although she was rather curious to see both her cousins again.

She caught sight of him in church on Christmas morning, where she decorously sat between Aunt Beryl and Uncle George, in the seats that had been theirs ever since Lydia could remember.

Bob, who was on the outside, did not look as though he had altered very much. He was still short and stocky, with hair combed straight back and plastered close to his head.

Olive, much taller than her brother, was dressed in thick tweed, with a shirt and tie, and the only concession to her invalidhood that Lydia could see, was a large and rather mangy-looking yellow fur incongruously draped across her shoulders.

Mrs. Senthoven's smaller, slighter figure was completely hidden from view by her offspring.

As they all met outside the church door, Lydia, in thought, was instantly carried back to Wimbledon again, and her sixteenth year.

"Hullo, ole gurl!" from Olive.

"Same to you and many of 'em," briefly from Bob, in reply to anticipated Christmas greetings.

"We'll all walk back to the Terrace together, shall we?" suggested Aunt Beryl, on whose mind Lydia knew that elaborate preparations for dinner were weighing. "Grandpapa will want to wish you all a Merry Christmas, I'm sure."

Aunt Evelyn, not without reason, looked nervous, nor did Grandpapa's greeting serve to reassure her.

"Why does little Shamrock bark at you so, my dear?" he inquired of Olive, with a pointed look at her short skirts. "I'm afraid he doesn't like those great boots of yours."

It was quite evident that Grandpapa's opinion of the Senthoven family had undergone no modification.

They sat round the fire lit in the drawing-room in honour of the occasion, and Aunt Beryl hurried in and out, her face flushed from the kitchen fire, and hoped that they'd "all brought good appetites."

"There's the bell, Lydia! I wonder if you'd go down, dear? I can't spare the girl just now, and it's only Mr. Almond."

Lydia willingly opened the door to her old friend, and received his usual, rather precise greeting, together with an old-fashioned compliment on the roses that London had not succeeded in fading.

She took him up to the drawing-room.

"Greetings of the season, ladies and gentlemen all," said Mr. Monteagle Almond, bowing in the doorway.

"Rum old buffer," said Bob to Lydia, aside.

She smiled rather coldly.

She felt sure that although the Bulteels and Miss Forster—who, after all, was the friend of Sir Rupert and Lady Honoret—might have accepted Mr. Almond and his out-of-date gentility, they would never have approved of Bob and Olive, with their witless, incessant slang.

"Now, then!" said Aunt Beryl, appearing in the doorway divested of her apron, and with freshly washed hands. "Dinner's quite ready, if the company is. George, will you lead the way with Evelyn?—Olive and Mr. Almond—that's right—now, Bob, you haven't forgotten the way to the dining-room—or, if you have, Lydia will show you—and I'll give Grandpapa an arm."

Aunt Beryl, for once, was excited and loquacious. Giving Grandpapa an arm, however, was a lengthy process, so that she missed the appreciative exclamations with which each couple duly honoured the festive appearance of the dining-room.

"How bright it looks!" cried Aunt Evelyn. "Now, doesn't it look bright?"

"Most seasonable, I declare," said Mr. Almond, rubbing his hands together.

"Oh, golly! crackers!"

"My eye, look at the mistletoe!" said Bob, and nudged Lydia with his elbow. Lydia immediately affected to ignore the huge bunches of mistletoe pendant in the window and over the table, and admired instead the holly decorating each place.

"A very curious old institution, mistletoe," said Uncle George, and seemed disappointed that nobody pursued the subject with a request for further information.

When they were all seated, and Grandpapa had leant heavily upon his corner of the table, and found a piece of holly beneath his hand, and vigorously flung it into the enormous fire blazing just behind his chair, Uncle George said again:

"Probably you all know the old song of the 'Mistletoe Bough,' but I wonder whether anyone can tell me the origin——"

"We'll come to the songs later on, my boy," said Grandpapa briskly. "Get on with the carving. Have you good appetites, young ladies?"

Olive only giggled, but Lydia smiled and nodded, and said, "Yes,

Grandpapa, very good."

"You needn't nod your head like a mandarin at me. I can hear what you say very well," said Grandpapa, and Lydia became aware that she had instinctively been pandering to the Senthoven view that Grandpapa was a very old man indeed, with all the infirmities proper to his age.

The Christmas dinner was very well cooked, and very long and very hot, and conformed in every way to tradition.

"Don't forget the seasoning in the turkey, George," said Aunt Beryl agitatedly. "There's plenty more where that comes from. Give Lydia a little more seasoning—she likes chestnut. Sausage, Evelyn? Sausage, Mr. Almond? Bob, pass the sauce-boat to your sister, and don't forget to help yourself on the way. There's gravy and vegetables on the side."

Everyone ate a great deal, and the room grew hotter and hotter, so that the high colour on Olive Senthoven's face assumed a glazed aspect, and the fumes from the enormous dish in front of Uncle George rose visibly into the air.

Presently Gertrude brought the plum-pudding, blazing in a blue flame, and with a twig of holly sticking from the top, and much amusement was occasioned by the discovery that several of the slices contained a small silver emblem. Mr. Monteagle Almond solemnly disinterred a thimble, and Bob, with a scarlet face, a wedding-ring.

Under cover of Olive's screams on the discovery of a three-penny bit on her own plate, he pushed the ring over to Lydia.

"I shall give it to you," he muttered gruffly.

After the plum-pudding, they ate mince-pies, and a little spirit was poured over each and a lighted match applied by Uncle George, Mr. Almond or Bob, Aunt Beryl and Aunt Evelyn, in accordance with the usage of their day, each uttering a small scream as the flame shot up. When the mince-pies were all finished, the dessert dishes were pulled out from under the piled-up heaps of crackers and holly surmounting them.

The dessert was also traditional—oranges, nuts, apples, raisins, almonds. Everybody avoided direct mention of these last from a sense of delicacy, until Mr. Monteagle Almond himself remarked humorously:

"I think I will favour my namesake, if the ladies will pardon an act of cannibalism."

Upon which everybody laughed a great deal and jokes were made, and Bob and Olive began to ask riddles.

In the midst of Bob's best conundrum, Grandpapa suddenly knocked loudly upon the table.

"Send round the port, George," he ordered solemnly. "Round with the sun ... that's right. The ladies must take a little wine, for the toasts."

Lydia knew what was coming. She had heard it every year, and the transition from jovial animal enjoyment to sudden solemnity always gave her a slight thrill.

Grandpapa raised his glass, and everybody imitated the gesture.

"The Queen! God bless her."

The sentiment was devoutly echoed round the table.

Then Uncle George said in a very serious way:

"Our absent friends."

And the toast was drunk silently, Aunt Beryl raising her handkerchief to her eyes for a moment as she did every year, in whose honour nobody knew.

After that healths were proposed and honoured indiscriminately. Mr. Monteagle Almond ceremoniously toasted Aunt Beryl, and Bob, looking very sentimental, insisted upon knocking the rim of his glass several times against the rim of Lydia's. Uncle George, noncommittally confining himself to generalities, proposed "The Fair Sex," and Grandpapa effectually prevented anyone from rising to reply by sarcastically inquiring which of the ladies present would act as representative for them all.

The room grew steadily hotter.

Lydia had enjoyed the resumption of old festive custom and also the additional importance conferred upon herself as a two days' visitor from London, but she found herself viewing the familiar Christmas rituals from a new and more critical angle.

She was inclined to wonder how they would strike the aristocratic boarding-house in Bloomsbury, or even the fashionable "young ladies" at Madame Elena's.

Surely it was an out-of-date custom to join hot hand to hot hand all round the table, and sing, "Auld Lang Syne" in voices made rather hoarse and throaty from food, and silently to pull each a cracker with either neighbour, hands crossed, and Uncle George saying, "One—two—three—all together, now—*Go!*"

Lydia felt mildly superior.

They adorned themselves with paper caps and crowns, Bob sheepishly self-conscious, Lydia critically so, and all the others merely serious. When no one could eat or drink anything more, Aunt Beryl said reluctantly:

"Well, then—shall we adjourn this meeting?" and they rose from the disordered table, now strewn with scraps of coloured paper from the crackers, dismembered twigs of holly, and innumerable crumbs.

"You gentlemen will be going for a walk, I suppose?" Aunt Evelyn suggested, as everyone hung about the hall indeterminately.

"That's right," said Grandpapa. "Get up an appetite for tea. And you'll take little Shamrock with you."

Little Shamrock, having been given no opportunity for over-eating himself, after the fashion of his betters, was careering round Uncle George's boots with a liveliness that boded ill for his docility during the expedition.

"We'll smoke a cigarette first, at all events," said Uncle George gloomily, and he and Mr. Almond and Bob went back into the dining-room again.

"You don't want to go for a walk, dear, do you?" said Aunt Beryl, and sighed with evident relief when Mrs. Senthoven shook her head in reply.

"Grandpapa?"

"The drawing-room is good enough for me," said Grandpapa, and Uncle George had to be called out of the dining-room again to help him up the stairs and instal him in his arm-chair by the window.

"I say, aren't you girls coming with us?" demanded Bob rather disconsolately, leaning against the open door of the dining-room with a half-smoked cigar in his mouth.

"You'll go too far for us," said Lydia primly.

"Let you and me go off somewhere on our own," struck in Olive. "I'm game for a toddle, if you are, but we don't want the men, do we?"

"You want to talk secrets—*I* know you," jeered Bob.

Lydia lifted her chin fastidiously and turned away.

Her cousins had not improved, she thought, and she was very angry when her dignified gesture inadvertently placed her beneath a beautiful bunch of mistletoe, hung in the hall by Aunt Beryl.

"Fair cop!" yelled Bob, and put his arm round her waist and gave her a sounding kiss.

She would not struggle, but she could not force herself to laugh, and she ran upstairs with a blazing face.

It was not that Lydia had any objection to being kissed, but that the publicity, and the scuffling, and the accompanying laughter offended her taste.

She felt almost as though she could have burst into angry tears.

"Are you two girls really going out?" Aunt Beryl inquired. "If so, I'll give you the key, Lydia. I'm letting the girl go home for the rest of the day, as soon as she's cleared up. The char's coming in to give her a hand with the washing-up."

"That's a *good* girl you've got hold of," Aunt Evelyn said emphatically. "She's been with you quite a time now, hasn't she?"

Aunt Beryl and Aunt Evelyn went upstairs, talking busily about the difficulty of training a servant really well, and then inducing her to remain with one. Presently, Lydia knew, they would go into Aunt Beryl's room, under pretext of looking at a paper pattern, or a new blouse bought at a clearance sale, and they would lie down on Aunt Beryl's bed, with eiderdowns and a couple of cloaks to keep them warm, and doze until tea-time.

Lydia herself felt heavy and drowsy, but nothing would have induced her to lie down upon her bed with Olive beside her. Instead, she put on her best hat and jacket, and a pair of high-heeled, patent-leather walking shoes, and took her cousin out into the mild damp of the December afternoon.

"What I call a muggy day," said Olive.

"Shall we go along the Front?" Lydia inquired.

"It's all those shoes of yours are good for, I should think," retorted Olive candidly. "Still the same old juggins about your clothes, I see?"

The Front—a strip of esplanade with the shingle and the grey sea on one side, beneath a low stone wall, and the green of the Public Gardens on the other—was almost deserted.

One or two young men in bowler hats and smoking Woodbine cigarettes hung round the empty band-stand, and an occasional invalid was pushed or pulled along in a bath-chair. Here and there a pair of sweethearts sat together in one of the small green shelters—the girl leaning against the man, and both of them motionless and speechless.

The sight of one such couple apparently gave Olive a desired opening.

"I say, what's all this about you falling in love with some chappie in London?" she demanded abruptly.

"I haven't fallen in love with anybody, that I know of," said Lydia coolly.

"But there was someone going after you, now, wasn't there?" urged Olive.

Lydia reflected.

"Who told you anything about it?" she demanded at last.

"Aunt Beryl told the mater."

Lydia perceived to her surprise that Olive did not, as she would have expected her to do, despise her cousin for "sloppiness." On the contrary, she appeared to be really impressed, and anxious to hear details from the heroine of the affair. Lydia did not resist the temptation.

She gave Olive a brief and poignant version of the tragedy.

There *had* been a man—a fellow-boarder at the great boarding-house in Bloomsbury that was always full of people, men and women alike. He was a foreigner—a distinguished sort of man—who had certainly paid Lydia a great deal of attention. Every-one had noticed it. Theatres, hansom-cabs, chocolates—he had appeared to think nothing too good for her. Certain of these attentions Lydia had accepted.

"Well, whyever not!" ejaculated Olive.

She worked hard all the week, and it was pleasant to have a little relaxation, and, besides, the Greek gentleman was most cultivated and clever—one had really interesting conversations with him about books. But——

Lydia paused impressively, really uncertain of what she was about to say. She was very seldom anything but truthful, and could not remember ever having told a direct lie since she was a little girl. Nevertheless, she did not want Olive to suppose her a mere dupe, the more especially as she felt perfectly certain that whatever she told Olive would be repeated to Olive's family, as nearly as possible word for word.

Lydia, therefore, said nothing untrue, but she rather subtly contrived to convey a desirable impression that, without any direct statements, should yet penetrate to Olive's consciousness. There had certainly been a mystery about the Greek. He was very uncommunicative about himself—even to Lydia herself. Then one day, after he had taken her out and been more attentive than ever, they had come in to find a foreign woman there who called herself his wife.

"Why, it's like a novel!" gasped Olive. "There's a plot exactly like that in a story called 'Neither Wife nor Maid.' Only the fellow turns out to be all right in the end, and the girl marries him."

"I should never have married Mr. Margoliouth," said Lydia haughtily.

"But of course he'd no right to carry on like that if he was married all the time," said Olive. "Men are rotters!"

Lydia gazed at her cousin thoughtfully.

"That woman *said* she was his wife," she remarked quietly.

"I say! d'you think it was all my eye and Betty Martin?"

"I don't know. But it was an awkward sort of position for him."

"Lord, yes!" said Olive more emphatically than ever, and Lydia felt that any humiliation attaching to the *débâcle* had been effectually transferred, so far as Olive's interpretation of it was concerned, from herself to the Greek deceiver.

"Of course, it doesn't matter to you, Lyd—a good-looking gurl like you," said Olive simply.

Lydia felt that after this she could well afford to change the conversation.

She made inquiries about Beatrice.

"Oh, just rotting about," said Olive discontentedly. "I wish she and I could do something for ourselves, the way you do, but the old birds wouldn't hear of it. Besides, I don't know what we could do, either of us. Bee plays hockey whenever she gets the chance, of course, and goes to all the hops. She's taken up dancing like anything."

"And haven't you?"

"Can't," said Olive briefly. "They're scared of me going off like the pater's sister. Chest, you know. But Beatrice is as strong as a horse. You know she's sort of engaged?"

"Who to?"

"The eldest Swaine boy—you remember Stanley Swaine? Nobody's a bit pleased about it, because they can't ever get married, possibly."

"No money?"

"Not a penny, and he's a perfect fool, except at games. He got the sack from the Bank, and now he hasn't any job at all. Bob says he drinks, but I daresay that's a lie."

"And does Beatrice like him?" said Lydia, rather astonished.

"Perfectly dotty about him. He's always hanging round—*I* think the pater ought to forbid him the house. But instead of that he comes in after supper of an evening, and he and Bee sit in the dining-room in the dark, and she comes up after he's cleared off with her face like fire and her hair half down her back. Absolutely disgusting, I call it."

Lydia was very much inclined inwardly to endorse this trenchant criticism.

She had never been so much aware of her own fastidiousness as she was now, on her return from the new surroundings which seemed to her so infinitely superior to the old. Really, it was terrible to think of how clever, fashionably-dressed Miss Forster, or haughty and disagreeable Miss Lillicrap, would have looked upon Olive Senthoven and her slangy, vulgar confidences.

As for the young ladies at Elena's, they would probably have refused to believe that anything so unrefined could be related to Lydia Raymond at all.

Nevertheless, Lydia Raymond expressed interest and even sympathy in all that Olive told her, and was conscious of feeling both pleased and flattered when, as they entered Regency Terrace again, Olive remarked with what, by the Senthoven standards, perilously approached to sentiment.

"I must say, ole gurl, I never thought you'd turn out such a decent sort."

They found Aunt Beryl, whose nap must after all have been a very short one, preparing a magnificent muffin-and-crumpet tea in the kitchen.

"Auntie! let me help you," Lydia cried.

"No, no. You go and take off your things."

Lydia pulled off her hat and jacket and laid them on the kitchen dresser.

"Are we using the blue tea-service to-day?" she asked calmly.

"But you're on a holiday, dearie! Don't you worry about the tea—I'll manage it. It's only to get the table laid in the drawing-room."

Lydia, however, carried her point. It would have made her feel thoroughly uncomfortable to see Aunt Beryl toiling upstairs with the heavy trays, and it would have looked, besides, as though she, Lydia, had grown to think herself too "fine" for household work.

So she carried the best blue china upstairs and set it out on the embroidered tea-cloth, and Aunt Evelyn, who was sitting with Grandpapa, looked at her approvingly and called her a good girl.

After tea she received other compliments.

They asked about her work in London, and Lydia told them about the great ledgers, and the bills and the invoices, and of how Madame Elena had practically said that she should leave Lydia in charge of the other girls, when she went to Paris to buy new models for Easter.

She also told them about the other young ladies, of Gina Ryott's good looks, and the cleverness and independence of little Rosie Graham, who lived in such nice rooms with a girl friend.

"And do they make you comfortable at the boarding-house?" Aunt Evelyn asked solicitously.

"Yes, very comfortable—and there were such nice superior people there. There was a Miss Forster, who played Bridge splendidly, and was great friends with a Sir Rupert and Lady Honoret, who lived in Lexham Gardens."

"Fancy!" Aunt Evelyn ejaculated. "I've seen Lady Honoret's name in print, too, I'm almost certain."

And the Bulteels were a nice family, Lydia said, with a clever son who went to Gower Street University.

"A great many clever folk in the world," said Mr. Monteagle Almond sentsentiously. "And no doubt you'll meet many of them in London. But I think, if you'll excuse personalities, that you'll find it's as I say—the true mathematical mind is a very rare thing in one of your sex."

Lydia's relations looked at her admiringly.

Only Grandpapa, with a detached expression, occupied himself in making a great fuss about Shamrock.

That night, when Lydia said good night to him, the old man fixed his eyes upon her with his most impish-looking twinkle.

"Why didn't you tell them about your romance, eh, Lyddie? The broken heart, and all the rest of it. You could have made a very pretty story out of it, I'm sure. You only told one-half of the tale when you were entertaining us all so grandly this evening. Always remember, me dear, whether you're listening to a tale or telling one: Every penny piece that's struck has two sides to it."